KILLER CALLING

KILLER
Calling

© 2016 Traci Tyne Hilton

Published by Proverbs 31 House

PO Box 3311 Vancouver WA 98668
www.proverbs31house.com

CHAPTER 1

"This is a tricky one." Flora handed a slim folder to Jane. "The client is panicking."

Jane Adler—recently married to Jake Crawford but as yet to have changed her name—sat across from Flora in the cluttered office of the Senior Corps of Retired Investigators. Driving rain from the day's storm smeared the drafty window. The heater had clicked on moments before with the dusty, but cozy, odor shared by all old buildings. She pulled her sweater a little tighter and opened the folder. It held a one-page dossier and an itinerary from Travelocity. At first glance, she saw nothing shocking. "What's the problem?"

"Teenagers." Flora chuckled, but after the last case, Jane wasn't so sure teenage problems were funny.

"Have you heard of the Trives family?"

"The name's familiar." Jane scanned the dossier again.

"It should be. They run an investment bank, and their name is on several buildings. Also, they participate in most of the major ministries in town. Victor and Lorraine Trives are passionate about the gospel."

"Yes! I know who you mean now. The little library at my old Bible school was the Trives Room."

"That sounds about right. The Trives have one daughter, Tory. Tory, for the last three years, has been outright hostile to anything having to do with God."

"Ouch." The single sheet of information about the Trives family also said Tory's volleyball team was the state champion and that she had had early acceptance to Pepperdine, but dropped out after one semester.

"It's to be expected. The poor girl is under a lot of pressure in this town. Everyone expects her to follow in the family footsteps, making and giving a lot of money. In my opinion, she's handling it fine, but my opinion doesn't matter." Flora had the age and experience to give weight to her opinion on teenagers.

"So what's the problem?"

"She has a new boyfriend, and they're going on a mission trip to Mexico next week."

"But that's great news!" Jane flipped to the itinerary. Two round-trip tickets to Los Angeles.

"I agree, but Mr. Trives doesn't. This new boyfriend has a Mohawk, tattoos, and he plays bass in a rock band."

"So…he's a youth pastor?"

Flora laughed. "No, he's a professional musician in a band. And he's a little older."

A little older. That hit a nerve with Jane. She could see, Mohawk aside, why Daddy Trives might worry.

"Mr. Trives believes completely that the only reason a tattooed, Mohawked thug—his words, not mine—would go to Mexico for a week is to smuggle drugs under the innocent guise of mission work." She sighed. "I think there's a high probability that he's worried over nothing, but as always, we need to treat the case with the same level of concern that the client does."

"Is that why it's tricky? Because odds are she's met a nice boy who has gotten her interested in Jesus again."

"Exactly. Odds are there is nothing going on that anyone has to worry about. Nonetheless, Mr. Trives has hired us to catch the boyfriend in action and protect Tory. It's impossible to prove a negative, Jane, so if this punk isn't smuggling drugs, the job is a whole lot harder than if he is. And if he is smuggling drugs from Mexico, you have the cartel to worry about."

Jane stared at Flora. All she could think of when she heard Mexican drug cartel was kidnappings, murders, and mass graves.

"The mission trip is a high school and college group from Freedom Faith Church—the exceptionally large one just outside of town. They are taking two weeks, so the kids going had to get time off of school. You'll fit in with that age group better than I would, so we're sending you."

"But it's not likely to be drugs, I mean, the odds are just super against it." Jane ran her finger up and down the folder. It sounded like the easiest hard job ever.

"I agree. If I thought there was any risk of you confronting a drug cartel, I wouldn't send you."

Jane exhaled. "Okay."

"But like I said, if they aren't there to smuggle drugs, you are going to have to prove it. Mr. Trives is a good man, but a hard one. It won't be easy."

"I see a ticket for Jake, too."

"Mr. Trives was very generous with the expenses. If Jake can't go, it's okay. But if he can, I think he'd be a real asset. You make a good team."

"I expect he can, but I'll ask." A well of pure happiness bubbled up in Jane. Flora was right. There wasn't much chance that the lovebirds had hitched a ride with a mission trip so they could smuggle drugs. She and Jake could buddy up with Tory and the new boyfriend, get to know them a little, and find out what had changed Tory's heart. That part would be simple. Then they could all focus on the ministry work and escaping the November rain.

It was like the world's perfect case. There was no way things could go wrong.

Travel to Mexico went as well as could be expected. Short plane ride, long drive. A good chance to observe and take notes, if nothing else.

The new boyfriend looked more than a little older. Chase McBane was short and stocky in a well-muscled way. He had a thick head of wiry black hair that he styled into a faux-hawk and stubble to match. If he was a day under twenty-five, Jane would be shocked.

She was shocked, anyway, but not just by his age. McBane wasn't a punk Portland kid in a band. McBane was bass player for

Rest from War—the most recent Christian band to have a single go viral with both Christian and secular audiences. Rest from War was kind of a big deal.

Jake and Chase seemed to hit if off right away, but Jane was hit hard by motion sickness. She attempted to introduce herself to Tory, to listen to the guy talk Jake and Chase were enjoying, but her stomach failed her. She took two little motion sickness pills and attempted to sleep.

When they finally arrived at the orphanage she dragged herself and her bags to the girls' dorm accommodations. She tried to keep up with the team but it was challenge.

Tory Trives threw her duffel bag on a top bunk and herself on a bottom. "We're done for the day, right?" She sounded beat.

"We're all meeting downstairs in the common room for a little supper and some instructions," one of the other team members, a girl who seemed older, offered.

Tory pressed her hands over her eyes. "It's after eleven." There was a plaintive whine in her voice, but her body language was screaming exhaustion.

Some people didn't travel well, and it looked like Tory and Jane were both on that unfortunate team.

Jane sat on the edge of another bottom bunk. She was awake, but just barely. A cool wind blew through the open window, refreshing after the hours in the closed up van with twelve youth and young adults.

She didn't even have the energy to wish she could hole away with Jake and make a plan of action. All she wanted was to sleep, and never look at food again. She took a deep breath and braced herself. "I'm with you, Tory, but we'd better go. If we don't they might sign us up for toilet duty."

"You have a point." Tory pulled herself to her feet with a groan. "If you can do it, I can." She offered Jane a hand. "I thought you were going to lose your lunch several times. I was so relieved when you fell asleep."

"Oh man, so was I." Jane followed Tory down to the common room. "It's been a while since I've travelled. I don't remember it being that bad when I was in youth group."

"It's hard to get old." There was a sympathetic tone to Tory's words that stung.

The team leader, Owen, stood in the center of a ring of folding chairs and the rest of the team, whom Jane had met on the plane, took their seats. Jake was sitting with Chase, laughing.

Jane lingered behind them, hoping to listen in without being noticed.

It didn't work. Chase jumped up. "Sit down, please." He waved at the seat he had just vacated. "Your husband is dying for your company."

Jake's eyes were showing signs of wear, but he smiled. Perhaps dying for bed, but not for company.

Jane sat.

"So you've been married, what, a year?" Chase asked.

"Just a couple of months." Jake put his arm over the back of the plaid couch.

Jane settled against him and closed her eyes. Must. Stay. Awake. Must observe. Must deduce. She yawned.

"Thanks for coming downstairs." Owen's voice woke Jane up, just a little. "I know it's very late, but you need to know two important things before tomorrow, and since you're here to learn those two things, I can tell you three or four less urgent, but still useful, things." He laughed.

No one else did, though Jake smiled.

There were two teams at the orphanage for the next two weeks. The team Jane and Jake had tagged along with was made up of a handful of older teens and college kids from Faith Freedom, one of Portland's mega churches. The other team was smaller and from a private school in little town called Kelseyville, California. But no matter where they were from, everyone had the same punch drunk, travel weary bleary eyes and posture.

"First and most important, the showers and bathrooms in the men's dorm building are out of commission. We are very sorry, but we had a deferred maintenance issue that couldn't be deferred any longer, and since our two groups are small, and short on men, the staff here decided now was the right time to do the work. So, men, you will be using the downstairs shower in the girls' dorm. Ladies, you get the upstairs. Second, breakfast is at 6:30, so you aren't getting much sleep tonight anyway. It's early mornings, but since we came here to serve, sleep would just be wasting our time, yes?" He laughed again.

"Gotcha." Chase nodded approval. He seemed so eager and positive. Unless he was a great actor and this was a total front, Jane couldn't see how Mr. Trives got a dangerous punk vibe from the Rest from War bassist.

"And the slightly less important things. Don't be late for your early breakfast. The orphanage will assign daily duties while you eat. A few of the staffers speak English, and they will be the ones working with you in the morning. That's your shot to ask questions because they go at it and go hard all day long. You might not catch them later if you decide to sleep in. And finally, we have chapel with the families every night. It's voluntary attendance, so not every family comes every night, but it's one of your best chances to get to hang out with the kids and to connect with the house parents who live here. The English-speaking staff will be around to translate. We meet in the volunteer lounge which you will find on the other side of the cafeteria."

Tory stood up. "Got it. Is that all?"

Owen consulted a paper. "Yes. The volunteer director would have met us here and given us the info himself, but not at this hour. If we eat at 6:30 you can only imagine what time they get up to get the meal ready for us." He folded the paper and slipped it into his jacket. "I'm bushed. Let's hit the hay."

Jake kissed Jane's cheek. "See you in the morning." He followed Owen to the men's side of the dorm.

Jane followed Tory back to their room and crashed. She thought about praying for energy and focus for the next morning but was dead to the world before she could turn her intention into action.

CHAPTER 2

Breakfast came early, but it was hot and delicious. Simple scrambled eggs and refried beans served with tortillas. Jane was rolling up her third when a handsome young man with thick black hair and dreamy eyes rapped a spoon on his coffee cup and got the attention of the group.

"*Buenos Días*." He smiled, but his eyes were moody, sad almost. "*Bienvenidos a la Casa de Esperanza.*" All eyes were on him. "Good morning. Welcome to the House of Hope. I'm Miguel, and I'm here with your work assignments." He continued his warm welcome by giving out assignments for the day.

Jane's first job at the orphanage—well, her first not-spying-on-Tory job—was in the preschool.

After breakfast and assignments and a commissioning style prayer send off, she found herself in a charming cement block building brightly painted and filled with happy young children.

She sat with a table of little girls, coloring pictures. The five girls had luminous black eyes, and black hair that also seemed to glow. Their tanned faces ranged from olive to coffee, and every one of them looked like the cover of a magazine. Little Pilar giggled into her fist and hid her picture. Monica turned red and looked around to see if any adults were watching, and then giggled too. The picture that had caused the laughter, as far as Jane could tell, was of a family, but all of the boys were standing on their heads.

"*Que paso?*" She had worked hard in college on her Spanish, but found herself at a loss for words more often than not. Pilar crumpled her picture up, laughing harder, her eyes closed and her cheeks pink from the effort. "*Nada, nada, nada.*" She took a deep breath, and started another picture.

The kids lived in big families in the orphanage, house parents caring for up to ten kids each, aged three to thirteen. Babies lived in the nursery, or *cuna* as they called it in Spanish. The teenagers moved to boys' and girls' dorms with a new set of house parents on their fourteenth birthday.

All of the kids Jane had met so far seemed happy and well adjusted. The first day on the job was turning out to be a real pleasure, coloring with the little girls, playing on the playground, but she wasn't working anywhere near Tory or Chase, and she was itching to find the evidence she needed to prove that Tory was really and truly born again and serving God.

The school bell that the orphanage used to mark the day's schedule rang cheerfully in the distance, announcing lunch.

"Pack it up, kiddos." Jane smiled and gathered up crayons. The kids had no idea what she was saying, but they knew what she was doing, and followed suit.

Lunch was served family style in a small cafeteria for the volunteers. The children ate with their mothers in their own houses.

Jane and Jake sat with their quarry. After a bilingual blessing by Miguel, the full-time volunteer coordinator, they passed around beans, tortillas, and cheese. A modest, but appreciated lunch.

"How's life in the baby nursery?" Chase asked his girlfriend.

Tory's eyes were half closed, and shadowed with thick, black liner. She shrugged. "Fine."

"It can't still be too early." Chase's tone was teasing. He stuffed half his burrito into his mouth at once.

"Jet lag," Jake offered. "I travel a lot for work and it can take a day or two to catch up."

"Baja is the same time zone as Portland." Jane nibbled her lunch and tried not to stare at Tory. Could she be using drugs while caring for the babies? That would be worse than awful, but it would explain the lack of eye contact and change in personality from yesterday.

"Tory was in New York a day and a half ago." Chase patted her back.

She leaned into him and yawned. "So. Tired." Her words were mumbled.

"You should go lie down." Jane wished Tory would look up. Red, bloodshot eyes would be a sign of drug use, right?

"Agreed," Chase said. "You should go sleep. Let the regular staff take care of the babies."

Tory shook her head. "I came to help. Just give me more coffee. There are babies who need snuggling, and I'm going to do it." These were the most words Jane had heard from her today, and they had clearly taken a good deal of effort.

Jane pondered the words. They weren't exactly emotionless, but they weren't enthusiastic either. Did she really want to snuggle babies? If she was using wouldn't she want that time alone in her dorm room to use more drugs? That's what people on drugs did, wasn't it? Get alone and get high? Jane realized her education was lacking in regards to how drug users functioned. She'd have to resolve that somehow. Maybe there was a book she could read.

"How are the big kids doing?" Jake asked her.

"Adorable and silly. Giggles and crayons are pretty much international. You guys have been working on the new classroom?"

"Yup," Chase responded. "Mixing cement and stacking blocks for foundation and walls. Makes me appreciate things like wood and nails."

"It's heavy work for a skinny guy like me," Jake said. "But it goes up pretty fast all things considered. Things being lack of cement mixing machines and trained crews to do the work."

Chase let a belly laugh loose that reminded Jane of her old uncle. "Jake and I are not the biggest and strongest our country has to offer, that's God's honest truth." Chase was twice as thick as Jake and all muscle, but he was no taller, only about 5 feet 8 or 9. "It's going to get hotter this afternoon. I'll be glad for the siesta hour." He stretched his arms out, and then draped one over Tory.

Lunch was over before Jane had had a chance to form any opinions. There just hadn't been enough to work with, and she had failed to lead the conversation. She'd have to work overtime during the siesta and pray that the chapel time in the evening offered some good spying.

One of the house mothers taught preschool to the littlest kids in the afternoon, and Jane joined her for the next shift. The children were gathered on a soft rainbow throw rug, sitting on their knees or cross-legged as the teacher sang to them about elephants balancing on a spider web. The tune was catchy and Jane hummed along as she wiped down the little round tables.

When she was done, she rinsed her rag in a sink at the back of the classroom. "What next?" Her coworker in the grub work was a young missionary named Ginger who lived at the orphanage full time.

"We'll take the kiddos out to play on the playground and then siesta," she said with a bright smile. "Preschool is the best job here. Color, play, tidy up a bit, play more, then take a nap. It's way better than maintenance or health care." She checked her watch. "Any minute now and we'll head outside." She leaned back on the counter, smiling at the kids and their teacher, her heart clearly filled with joy.

The children seemed to enjoy their playground time, laughing in the sun, giggling in the shade. Against the wall of the school house, in a shady spot, three girls no older than four attempted headstands. One stout girl with thick pigtails made it work, but laughed so hard she slid down the side. A thin girl with huge black eyes shook her finger at her with a heavy frown on her face and then broke into giggles.

Their laughter made Jane laugh. Sure, she was here to do Mr. Trives' bidding, but she could enjoy the kids, enjoy their silliness and be thankful for the opportunity to serve them all the same. The preschool teacher joined the girls in the shade. She knelt down eye to eye with them and spoke softly.

The stout girl who could do her headstand pursed her lips in anger.

The other two took hands and skipped off.

The teacher led the upset girl quietly to the swings and engaged her in a new activity.

Jane had always heard that a grassy playground could be as hard as concrete. But try to explain that to a four-year-old who wanted to do gymnastics.

In the distance Jane spotted Tory and Owen, their team leader. They seemed to meet in passing. Tory's body language was aloof, seeming to look past Owen. He gestured, like he was trying to get her attention. But Tory didn't seem to notice and she walked at a fast clip around the corner.

They hadn't had a full tour of the grounds, but Jane was going to have to find out what was behind the volunteer dorms that might interest Tory.

Eventually dinner rolled around. The kitchen crew served up a cafeteria standard—chicken patties and mashed potatoes, differing from the Northern version only by the amount of spice the cooks preferred.

Jane and Jake cornered Tory and Chase again, sidling next to them at the table until their quarry was situated at the very end of the bench and could talk to no one else.

"How was the rest of your day?" Jane asked Chase.

He grinned. "Pretty good. Got to get dirty. I always like that."

"Same." Jake scooped a big spoonful of refried beans onto his plate. If beans were served at every meal, Jane wasn't sorry they weren't sharing a room.

"I'm exhausted, but I made it through the day without sneaking in a nap," Tory volunteered. "Even during siesta."

"Good job. It's the only way to get over jet lag. Power through it." Chase attempted to encouraged her.

"Truth," Jake agreed.

As the only one without recent jet lag experience, Jane just smiled.

"But it wasn't easy rocking soft warm babies all day. Seriously, there isn't a worse job in this whole place for a person desperate to stay awake."

Jane laughed. "It sounds like the nicest torture ever."

"Correct. As much as I could spend all week doing it, I hope I get to be a little more active tomorrow." She yawned deeply, her hopeful words at odds with the shadows under her eyes and the sag in her shoulders.

"You guys on construction are stuck with that one job for two weeks, right?" Jane asked.

"Mm hmmm," her husband responded through a mouth full of burrito.

"But the rest of us will rotate our way around the orphanage, so hopefully I'll get a chance with those nice babies."

Chase nudged Jake with his elbow. "Already with the baby talk. Watch out, buddy."

Jane blushed, but smiled. "No way. I've got my career to establish first."

"And what career is that?" Chase asked, a look of genuine interest on his face.

Jane froze. Crap. She was a detective. What could she say that wouldn't get his suspicions up?

"She's in criminal justice," Jake volunteered.

Always ready and so smooth with words. Jane loved him.

"What branch?" Chase directed his question to Jane.

"I just graduated, but I'm hoping to work privately, if possible. Investigations and stuff." She trailed off wishing she could rewind dinner.

"I want to send her to law school. She could be my very own personal Matlock."

"Awesome." Chase nodded with approval.

Tory hadn't spoken, but gave Jane a pointed side eye.

Jane had absolutely said too much.

Tory stood up with her tray. "I'm beat." She dropped the mostly full tray off at the kitchen window and left.

They had a little time to themselves after dinner. Jane took her husband by the hand and led him on a leisurely stroll around the dorm buildings just to see what might have drawn Tory that direction.

The dorms were located on the west side of the property, removed from the family homes and the school buildings. They were surrounded by sandy, undeveloped ground. No lawn, no landscaping. It wasn't bleak, really, just a sign that the money donated to the orphanage was spend on the kids, rather than the tourist-volunteers. The land behind the dorms was just a parking lot. Several beat up vans and two tractors were stationed there at the moment. The parking was fenced and gated, the only neighbor a large farm and a two lane dirt road.

"So perhaps she snuck around here to meet someone," Jane murmured.

"Tory snuck around here?"

"Yeah, sorry." She caught him up with Tory's earlier disappearance. "I wanted to see what might have been of interest back here. It looks like a pretty good meeting place if someone was coming here to pick up or deliver."

"Bummer. I was really hoping Victor Trives was off his rocker. I like that Chase guy. Pretty cool for a rock star."

CHAPTER 3

Miguel, the handsome orphanage volunteer coordinator with the remarkable eyes, stood at the front of a cozy, shabby room filled with overstuffed outdated sofas. He had a huge grin on his face. Two of the resident families, with all of their kids were crowded onto the sofas, small children on their moms' and dads' laps, big kids draped over the arms of the sofas, and sitting on the shag rug covered concrete floor, their heads rested against their parents' knees.

The volunteers straggled in looking hot and tired. There weren't enough seats for everyone, so the volunteers collapsed into any available spot.

"I am very excited about chapel tonight." Miguel clapped his hands together, like a kid on Christmas Eve. "It is not every day I have an announcement like this." He turned his gaze to Owen, the fearless leader of Jane's team. Owen nodded, also smiling.

"Tonight we're going to have a time of singing, a whole hour of praising God. And to lead it, we are very blessed. I would like to introduce you to Chase McBane, the bassist from Rest from

War! He is going to lead our worship team tonight." He looked to Chase, but Chase was head down, focused on tuning his guitar.

The other volunteer team erupted in loud applause. Jane's team clapped politely. The families looked confused.

Miguel repeated it all again in heavily accented Spanish. The parents clapped politely. The kids were getting wiggly.

It appeared that Rest from War didn't enjoy the same kind of fame down here that it did back home. On some level, Jane figured that had to disappoint both Miguel and Chase. But she was also disappointed. Singing for an hour wouldn't help her pick up any clues.

Fortunately, Chase didn't ask anyone to stand, and had the good sense to pick songs that the regular worship crew at the orphanage knew. The singing was a bit like Pentecost—Spanish and English colliding—but it was perfectly joyful and spirit-filled.

Miguel joined in the worship. He had a high voice when he spoke and sang that seemed to fit his tall, slender frame. He blended well with Chase's deeper but still smooth voice. Despite her disappointment, Jane found herself refreshed and thankful for the hour to focus on God.

Tory, she noted, had fallen asleep.

At breakfast the next day, Jane sat next to Tory, whose eyes were still shrouded in deep shadows almost like black eyes. They were also bloodshot.

Ginger from the preschool, who Jane had worked with the day before, joined them. "Worship was great last night, wasn't it?" She was cheerful and very awake for this early in the morning.

"I loved it." Jane sipped her coffee. "I was hoping for more of a devotional time, but it turned out that was just what I needed."

"You can count on Miguel to get it right. I swear his instincts are spot on." She had a far-away look in her eye, Jane suspected she might be crushing on her boss.

"What did you think?" Jane asked Tory.

Tory looked up from her eggs. "It was nice." She sounded sincere, but exhausted. What drugs could she be doing that would knock her out for the whole day like that and still have her in bad shape this morning? Jane needed to find time to call Rocky and Flora to help her figure it out.

"You don't look so hot." Ginger directed her question to Tory. "Are you okay?"

"As well as could be expected." Tory stood up with her half-finished plate. "I'll feel better after a shower."

If she was going to sneak away now for a shower, she'd miss her assignment. Jane suppressed a smile. That meant Tory would need someone to update her on the day's plan, and that someone could be Jane. Perhaps today she'd get lucky and crack the nut that was Tory Trives.

Jane was assigned to the bathrooms, and Tory to the orchard. "Want to switch?" Tory asked when Jane delivered the news in their dorm.

"Are you kidding?" Jane laughed.

"I'm allergic to something out here. Don't know what it is, but it's killing me. If I could clean toilets instead of work outside it would help a lot."

Jane had been very disappointed not to get assigned together, but allergies explained a lot. The black shadows under her eyes could easily be "allergy shiners" and the bloodshot eyes the result of some kind of pollen. The sleepiness . . . it all sort of made sense.

And yet, bathroom cleaning was done pretty much by yourself, whereas working in the orchard was a group activity. If Tory wanted to get loaded, or make a purchase, or a delivery, or whatever, it would be a lot easier to do while on bathroom duty.

Jane quickly weighed the situation and went for it. "Of course. Please. You don't have to beg to clean toilets for me."

Relief washed over Tory. "Thank you so much."

"No problem. Do you need anything? I'm sure the nurse has some kind of allergy meds."

Tory shook her head. "I've got everything I ought to be taking, but the beast out here is strong. Thanks for trading. Don't forget your sunscreen."

The orphanage maintained an extensive almond orchard. Harvesting, processing, and sales of the nuts contributed funds for the families, work experience for the teenagers, food for the children, and even almond milk for those who might need it. It was a relatively genius operation, and impressed Jane in a very "give a man a fish" kind of way. The place wasn't just shelter for kids, but a real life experience, raising them, and giving them so many unique opportunities.

Her work day began with a tour of the processing facilities which were empty, that work being done for the season. Then they went out to the orchard itself to do simple fall tasks like raking the leaves and turning the compost barrels. There wasn't much to do at this point in the season, so Enrique, the orchard supervisor, entertained them with the history of the orchard and the many ways it blessed their community before setting them on their jobs.

For a while, Jane let herself get lost in the wonder of service and mission work.

Then the sound of Chase's booming laugh floated to her from the nearby worksite. From her spot at the wire mesh compost barrel she was in the middle of turning, she could see the men building.

Jake stayed in one place, stirring something with a big shovel, two other men did the same, and a bevy of other workers hustled to haul, stack, scrape and pour their way to a firm foundation.

This new building was the farthest away from family life, and was slated to be a kind of study hall for older students, tutors, and visiting pastors who could take seminary type classes from Dr. Ben Rodriguez, who ran the whole show.

Movement to the side, in grassy area that was mostly empty, caught Jane's eye. Someone dressed in black, running to the work site. It looked like Tory, she wasn't familiar enough with her to identify her with confidence

She tracked the runner, hoping she'd grab Chase's attention, but the girl skirted the work site and continued into the back of the orchard where Jane lost sight of her, though the trees were well tended and far from densely packed.

"Did you see that?" Jane asked the girl nearest her who was raking.

"Hmmm?" She looked up and pulled an earbud out. "What was that?"

"I thought I saw someone run into the orchard . . . just wondering if you saw her."

She shook her head and plugged herself back in. Jane was pretty sure the earbuds and device were verboten during work hours, but wasn't planning on turning her partner in for the infraction.

Little tasks like turning the compost didn't take long, but raking the fifty acres of almond orchard would take all week most likely. The solitary nature of the work made it the last pick on Jane's wish list. It also felt somewhat like busy work, though the orchard manager swore that raking would protect the younger trees. Jane thought leaving the leaves would have helped prevent water evaporation but she didn't say anything, since she was as far from a farmer as they come.

Young men were high up in cherry pickers—well, almond pickers—attached to small tractors, "sanitizing" the trees by removing almonds that had not fallen so they wouldn't become hosts to parasites. That seemed like real work, and Jane would have liked to try it, both because it looked legitimate and because she'd have a better view of where her black-clad runner had gone.

None of the short-term volunteers were offered a spot on the picker, and Jane went back for lunch with the rest of them, disappointed in the quality of both ministry and detective work she had done.

Jane tried to sit next to Tory at lunch, but a couple of overly enthusiastic youth nudged her out of the way. The two girls, a blonde and a brunette who Jane had been introduced to but couldn't remember, huddled close and talked fast.

Tour. Travel. Tom Henry. Rock Star. Those were a few of the words Jane could pick out of the conversation, so clearly they were enamored with Rest from War and wanted to hear everything Tory had to say about life on the road and the handsome lead singer of the band.

Tory scrunched her nose up, but answered questions as fast as they hit her.

None of the building crew had come in yet, so Jane moved over and sat next to her team leader, Owen.

"How was your second day at work?" he asked.

"It's a beautiful day to be outside." Jane sipped her *café con leche* and decided half milk and half coffee was a pretty genius arrangement. "But it's kind of lonely in the orchard. I wouldn't have minded another day with the preschool."

"You're a people person. I can tell. I bet I can get you an afternoon job you'll like better."

"Oh I don't want to be a bother . . ." Though it was true she didn't want to be a bother, she would love with all her heart to get moved.

"Not a problem. There's a group of women sewing school uniforms today who could always use an extra hand."

"Sounds like this isn't your first trip to the orphanage."

"Nope. I come twice a year. I'd come more if I had more time." Owen dug into his lunch—stewed chicken in some kind of red sauce, refried beans, tortillas, and a refreshingly crispy and cold iceberg lettuce salad. He balanced a bit of all of it onto a fork and had it in one bite.

"Thanks for letting Jake and I tag along on your trip." She knew that he knew why she was along, and appreciated it.

"Coming here is good for the soul." He put his fork down and gave her an uncomfortably sincere look. "It doesn't really matter what brings a person here. Being here is what matters."

Jane rubbed her lips together and nodded. Sure. Exactly. Missions. Serving. She agreed totally with the sentiment, but the delivery was a bit much. "So how did you connect with a rock star like Chase McBane?"

"Same way I connected with you." He scooped himself seconds on the chicken. "A call came from the Trives organization. No one in nonprofit says no to a Trives."

"Victor Trives called?"

Owen shook his head. "Someone from the office did. There's always room for more, so we added Chase and Tory to the roster. And then, two days later we added you and Jake." He grinned. "A couple of Crawfords, a Trives, and the bassist from Rest from War? Not bad from a fundraising point of view, wouldn't you say?"

Jane stared at him, shocked. She hadn't considered that before. That being a "Crawford" meant something kind of like being a "Trives" did. Obviously not to the same extent. The Crawford family wasn't building libraries for universities or anything, but still...

"Just don't be surprised when the appeals letters start showing up in your mailbox."

She laughed. "I've only been a Crawford for a few months. I'm not used to being a mark yet."

Owen smiled. "May the pleasure of having much to give never grow old." He cleaned his plate and excused himself.

Someone's assistant had made a point to book Chase and Tory on this mission trip. But how had Tory and Chase found out about the team Owen was taking? Sheer luck? Or were they involved with the church who organized it?

Jane scooted down the bench to sit closer to the other team members, but lunch was ending, and no one did more than exchange hellos with her before they left.

The volunteer coordinator was happy to let her join the house mothers in the sewing room. Schoolchildren in Mexico were required to wear uniforms. The house mothers did all of the sewing for their own children and, when that work was done, a few of them volunteered their time to sew uniforms for other kids in the area. The community was very poor and lack of uniform meant no education for the children. One simple outfit could make a lifelong difference, both for the child and the village as a whole.

Jane didn't know how to sew. Nonetheless, she settled in with the mothers, ready to get to know the community better.

Perhaps while they sewed they would gossip about the trouble the youths in the area were getting into . . . like drugs. There was always a chance that this afternoon chat session over sewing needles and plaid polyester would give her the clue that opened her case up.

But even if there wasn't any good gossip, there was a bathroom not far from the sewing room, and Tory ought to be coming by to clean it. Also, the room had big picture windows that looked onto the courtyard, so Jane also ought to be able to keep an eye on Tory's comings and goings.

The mothers spoke fast and furious in Spanish and Jane was having a hard time keeping up. In fact, there were so many unfamiliar words she suspected they were speaking a dialect that was very far removed from the Castellan-influenced school Spanish she had worked so hard on.

Jane was established at a table, pinning a pattern on some dark blue plaid that would become a knee length pleated skirt when it was finished.

One of the mothers sat across from her with a long pile of sturdy string in her lap. As she talked with the other ladies she handled the strands of string one by one, running her fingers over them as though they made her happy. The strings had series of knots in them that looked like they'd make a good sensory activity for small children. Jane watched for a while, and then asked, "*Que es eso?*" nodding at the string.

The house mother sighed in a satisfied kind of way and said, "*Es cultura, sólo cultura.*" The other mothers nodded in agreement.

Just culture?

"*Que significa?*" Jane asked. What does it signify?

The house mother explained at length in Spanish. Jane understood enough to know that the strings were some kind of ancient art that the kids liked to see.

The women changed the subject to uniforms, but Jane kept her eye on the woman with the strings, attracted by the rhythmic nature of the activity. It looked as though the act of touching and knotting the strings was the actual art, rather than the finished product being the goal. Jane was mesmerized. In all of her classes on culture and Latin America, Jane hadn't seen or heard of anything like this.

She snipped the plaid fabric and watched the mother knot her strings, as Tory came in.

"*Donde está el baño?*" Her accent was laughably American and, indeed, the mothers did laugh, but they pointed out the bathroom and Tory tugged her bucket of spray bottles and rags into the room they pointed out.

Now Jane had Tory just where she wanted her. She walked to the bathroom as casually as possible, though the women sewing didn't pay any attention to her. She let herself in and shut the door behind her. Tory was sitting on the closed toilet with her head in her hands.

"You doing okay?" Jane asked.

Tory looked up and scowled. "No. But what does it matter? I'm not here for me."

"Are you sure I can't do anything for you?"

"You could please just leave me alone." She pressed her hands against her eyes. "I'll adjust in a day or two."

"Do you want to switch? I'll finish the bathrooms and you could help sew. It might be easier on you."

Tory took a little while to answer. "If you want to clean the bathrooms, go for it." She stood slowly and carefully as though nursing a headache, and left. Jane followed her out and watched her cross the courtyard, not in the direction of the dorms.

Another misplayed hand. Jane picked up the spray bottle labeled "bleach" and mentally kicked herself. Now she couldn't get any gossip from the mothers, and she couldn't watch the courtyard for any shenanigans by Chase and Tory. At this rate all she'd get to do in Mexico was mission work.

CHAPTER 4

Then next morning, after Miguel handed out work assignments, he paused, a look of sorrow slowly marking his face. "Thank you so much for coming here to serve us and to live with us, for even so short a time." He cleared his throat. "Here at the orphanage we go through the same range of human experience that you do at home. This evening instead of chapel, we're having a memorial service for Claude Marshall, just for the families. He lived and worked with us for ten years. We are so grateful for his time here, and the life of service that he lived. He was fifty-three years old, far too young to die, but he had a heart condition, so while we didn't expect him to die, it also wasn't a shock." He cleared his throat again, clearly trying not to cry. "Claude was the head of our maintenance crew and kept all of our buildings and machines running. As it happens, two days before you arrived, he passed away. Later this week we will have a very formal funeral service. I hope you will all join us for it. It will be a very traditional goodbye from his adopted town of El Ruego, Mexico, and all of us here in the *Casa de Esperanza*."

Jane hated to think of herself as coldhearted, and knew that she really needed to check herself, but the funeral seemed like just another thief, stealing the little time she had to get into Tory's head and move her investigation forward. Fortunately, Tory had skipped breakfast, so Jane could at least find her to let her know what her work assignment was.

Jane found the daughter of one of Portland's leading Christian families in the dorm lying with a washcloth over her head. She sat on the floor next to her. "Are you okay?" She asked.

Tory groaned.

"Are you sure I can't get the nurse for you?"

Tory groaned again.

"Hey, what's going on?"

Tory removed the washcloth and sat up. "Jane, these allergies are seriously killing me." She gritted her teeth and squeezed her eyes shut. "I told Chase that it would be complete misery if I came with him." She ended her complaint on an especially whiney note and then laid back down and slipped the washcloth back over her forehead.

"You didn't want to come?"

"It's not that I didn't want to be here, but I knew I couldn't hack it. I know my limitations."

"Are you sure I can't get the nurse?"

"Forgot about it. It's a sinus headache. Aspirin won't help and I've already got allergy medicine. There's nothing you can do. Just go away and leave me alone."

"I could maybe pray for you."

Tory sighed heavily. "It's a sinus *headache*. If you want to pray for me, could you do it somewhere else so that I can maybe lie here in silence?"

"Yes, of course. I'm sorry." Jane slipped out of the dorm as quietly as she could and prayed as she wandered back towards the dining room. It was pretty fishy kind of headache if normal headache medicine couldn't help. And it was yet another day where Tory would be free to slip away if that was what she was here for, since she wouldn't be checking into a job.

Jane spent the morning in the cafeteria with a couple of American teenagers, mopping and scrubbing. Their chatter was entirely about Rest from War and how old Miguel the volunteer coordinator might be and if he might be single.

During siesta, she found Jake loitering in the doorway of the volunteer lounge. He jerked his head in the direction of the open field. Jane nodded and they walked that way. "What's the word on Chase?"

"Glad you asked." Jake took her hand in his. "He didn't show up for his work job this morning. I asked—you're welcome— Owen said Chase had a prearranged thing today to hang out with fans in Ensenada."

"That's like an hour way away. How could he fit a trip there and back in the morning?"

"It's not just the distance that makes it weird. Remember the way the families acted when Miguel told them Chase was a member of Rest from War?" Jake pressed his point.

"Yes, with confusion."

"Rest from War is just not as famous here as back home. They are too new, too American. Too religious. You and I both know that Christian music, books, film, all of that stuff doesn't have much of a market outside of the U.S. So where'd he find fans to meet with?"

"He didn't, did he?" Jane turned and began to walk back towards the orphanage.

"Of course not, so what was he doing?"

"That can't too hard to discover. First we find out how he left, then where he ended up. That pretty much reveals what he was doing." Jane was headed toward the main business office of the orphanage. "But while we sort out these little details, I am trying to get a grip on what's going on with Tory. She claims she has allergies so bad that she can't get out of bed, and nothing relieves her symptoms."

"Ouch."

"Sure, if it's true. But what's handier than not having to work on a work trip, if you are actually here to sneak around selling drugs?"

"Your evidence that she's not here to work?"

"That's the sticky point. At least this morning she was actually in bed. If sickness is an excuse to sneak away, she hasn't snuck yet, as far as I can tell." Jane paused in front of the office. "But if she's that allergic to Mexico, why did she bother to come?"

Marcia, the receptionist in the cement block office building was graciousness herself but said that as far as she knew, Chase left in his own vehicle. He had popped in to say a friendly goodbye, but hadn't given her any information about where he was going or with whom. For all she knew, he had gone alone.

Jane kicked at the dusty sidewalk in frustration as she walked back with Jake. "I guess if he took the team van, Owen, our fearless leader, would know."

"Why don't I ask about it while you go see if Tory is sticking to her sick in bed scheme." Jake planted a big fat kiss on his wife and sprinted across the campus.

Jane poked her head in the dorm. Tory was asleep in bed.

Instead of chapel, Owen gathered all of the volunteers together in the lounge where the volunteers met and where they had had their casual concert.

He led a brief Bible study followed by some singing, led by the guy in charge of the team from California. They were both heartfelt, and took some time to pray for the residents on the loss of their friend, but Jane's heart wasn't in it, and when they were released on their own recognizance, Jane was relieved.

She and Jake cornered Chase, Jane on his left side and Jake his right, and steered him out to a patio with benches and a good view of the night sky.

"Tory's sure not feeling well," Jane said. "Do you know anything that could help her feel better?"

"She told me it was going to be like this," Chase said, "but I didn't believe her. Part of me thought she was exaggerating and the other part thought since this is mission work, God would make sure her allergies didn't bother her."

Jane laughed. "It seems like he would, don't you think?"

"It's a beautiful night," Jake said.

"It's a bummer Tory can't see it." Chase added, "I just love that girl so much."

"How long have you known her?" Jake asked.

"About six months. We met back stage at a fundraising concert in Chicago."

"She sure travels a lot for a student," Jane murmured. She tried to walk the line between curious in a friendly way and nosy. She knew an awful lot about Tory's school history, but as it was a high school and college trip, she was playing dumb.

"Oh, she's not in school. She's under the assumption that since there's no end to Trives money she won't ever have to work...or that she'll just work for her daddy."

Jane laughed. "Nice life."

Jake frowned. "Tempting life."

"You would know," Chase said. It sounded like Jake and Chase had had a chance to catch up on their backstories.

"Yup, but I went to school. I couldn't let myself give in to the temptation."

"What about you, Chase? Did you go to school?" Jane asked.

"Yeah," he said. "Community college anyway. I was studying music. Then the guys and I got our record deal and I quit, but just for now. Fame doesn't usually last."

"Invest wisely, son." Jake put on fatherly tones that didn't match his youthful look.

Jane considered Chase's situation. Two years of community college, then the record deal. Rest from War had been on the scene for about two years now. Chase must be younger than he looked.

"How did you guys hook up with the orphanage?" Jane asked.

Chase hesitated for the first time. No glib answer at hand. The hesitation turned into a long awkward pause. Finally, he answered, "My baby sister grew up here."

"No kidding?" Jake asked, "Did you parents adopt her?"

"Yeah, they did. She's sixteen now. We were finally able to sign the papers when she was ten."

"That's really cool, but I thought the point of this orphanage was that kids grew up here with the families," Jane said.

"They do, if they are citizens of Mexico. Sis lived here but she had no known extended family, no Mexican papers. When my parents came through about twelve years ago she was just a wee little thing and the orphanage didn't know what to do with her."

"What do you mean she didn't have any papers?"

"It's complicated. Sis was born in America, in San Diego, but her mom couldn't make it work there so she came back to

Ensenada, just her and the baby. She either abandoned Sis or she died, we don't know which, but someone left Sis here, with an American birth certificate, father's name blank."

"They don't know who left the baby here?"

"Nope. Not a clue. And they looked. They do their very best to keep everything on the up and up around here. Legal paperwork can be a nightmare and the work they do is too important to mess around."

"Have you come before?"

"This is my first visit. Sis never wanted me to come. I think she has good memories of it, but I think now she just wants to be a . . . McBane, you know? Just a normal American girl. And then again, maybe her memories of the orphanage are too good. Maybe she didn't want to leave. She really didn't have choice. As far as the organization was concerned, anyway. She's lucky she didn't end up on the streets. A lot of kids do."

"It's kind of an incredible story," Jane said. "When she's older I think she'll really appreciate the miraculousness of it."

"I hope so. She's a great kid. I could not ask for a better kid sister. She's a full six years younger than me, but she seems much more mature than that. And she's beautiful too. I'm not home as much as I should be. She needs a big brother to scare the boys away. She's got that olive skin, but huge green eyes. Girls shouldn't be that pretty." He laughed with brotherly affection.

"Do she and Tory get along?"

"They actually haven't met yet."

"Oh, no kidding?"

"My parents live in St. Louis. Tory's been around with me, here there and everywhere while I tour, but we haven't been home yet. It's not been long, just six months, but when you've found the one, you've found her, you know?"

"I do," Jake said.

"What made you decide to come down this time?" Jane asked.

He paused again, another long awkward wait. "It was just time."

They sat in the quiet, under the stars, for a while longer. Maybe being a star made Chase used to being interviewed. After his first hesitation, where he decided if he was going to play along or not, he certainly acted like their Q and A had been perfectly normal and not invasive. And he hadn't shown the slightest interest in learning more about them.

Eventually Jane stood to go. Her fingers laced loosely through Jake's.

"Can I come, too?" he asked, a hint of desire in his low tones.

"Not just yet." She had decided to go check on Tory. Maybe she was feeling well enough to answer some questions . . . just enough to see if her story would match up with Chase's.

The walk through the quiet, moonlit orphanage grounds was lovely, and Jane was in a mellow, contemplative mood when she entered the dorm. She was ready to casually get to know Tory better.

Unfortunately, Tory was gone.

CHAPTER 5

Tory made it to breakfast looking much more with it than the previous two days. She was assigned to the *cuna* to care for the babies so she didn't offer to switch Jane's toilet duty. She claimed she had given in and gone to the nurse the night before.

She also managed to sit with some of the other team members from the college group. Jane herself hadn't put any effort into getting to know the rest of the team, and was suddenly aware that she might be contributing to a bad vibe. No one wanted their mission trip ruined by snotty team members.

"Morning," She greeted a perky blonde sitting next to her.

"*Buenos días,*" The girl said with a smile. "You look like you're feeling better."

"Of, for sure. But the trip over was rough on me!" Jane sipped her coffee and hoped the idea of prolonged travel sickness would help the other teammates forgive her for her snobbish seeming attitude.

"You and your boyfriend seem to be hanging out with Chase McBane a lot." The girl said his full name with a note of awe. "Have you known him long?"

"Er, my husband and I, we just met Chase and Tory." She wasn't sure how the marriage was supposed to fit into her fake backstory. Probably Flora hadn't wanted them to pretend to be single. That would be a weird thing to lie about. Christians got married in college all the time.

"Husband? That's cool. How long have you been married?"

"Just a couple of months."

"Wow! And you are already on a mission. You guys rock. I hope I can have a husband like that someday."

Jake was on the other end of the table trying to balance an orange on his thumb. Jane laughed. "He's fun, that's for sure."

"What job did you have yesterday?" the blonde asked.

"Cafeteria duty, you?"

"I was in the preschool, but you know what was weird?"

"What?" Jane only gave the girl half an ear. Tory and Chase were secluded in a back corner and she could almost make out what Tory was saying, but not quite.

"Well, see the little boys and girls were kind of fighting, play fighting, I think, I can't be sure because they kind of talk baby talk Spanish and while I'm basically fluent there are like, subtleties, you know? Things you don't really learn in a classroom. But they were arguing and one of the little boys pushed one of the girls, the teacher saw it, and she punished the girl."

"Oh, that's too bad." Jane had almost deciphered Tory's last sentence while the blonde rambled on. Something about . . . congestion, probably.

"I thought it was odd since the boy pushed her, but it got weirder. When the house parents came to take the kids home for the afternoon, the teacher pulled aside the parents of the little girl and there was a big lecture between the teacher and the parents. The dad put the little girl in the corner, on her head, like for a headstand. She was bawling, and her face was turning red and she couldn't really keep herself upright. And every time she fell over they gave her a spanking. I've never seen anything like it. It was . . . I don't know. I didn't like it." The blonde's face drained of color. "But it was the housefather, you know? So it must have been okay. Then again, boy was the one who pushed the girl and he didn't get into any trouble at all."

Jane turned her full attention back to the blonde. "They spanked her when she fell over?"

"Yeah. That's not normal, is it?"

"No, it's not. Did they do this in the classroom?"

The girl blushed. "No . . . I followed them home, at a discreet distance, and watched through the window."

"So they did this in private . . ."

"It kind of looked like that."

"I think you need to tell someone. I don't think that sounds healthy."

"But who would I tell? And what would I say?"

"Let's go to the head office, and . . . just say everything you said to me."

Jane was late getting to her job for the day.

The blonde, who introduced herself as Riley, repeated everything she had said for the director of the orphanage, Dr. Ben Rodriguez.

Rodriguez an older man, and American, but he had lived in the small village near Ensenada for three decades running the orphanage. He seemed tired. "I will look into it."

"But it does seem strange, right? Like, he shouldn't have been hitting that little girl, and making her stand on her head while she was bawling and her face was turning red? That seems like psychological abuse. All the blood rushing to her head, and the snot, you know how it is when you are crying hard, right? I bet she couldn't even breathe. It was scary to watch." Riley was leaning forward, almost aggressively, eager to make her point understood. "It can't be okay that he did that. Do you want me to bring him in here? I can go get him. I would recognize him really easily."

"I said I would look into it. You're excused." He closed his mouth, his lips a thin line, his deep-set eyes half closed.

Jane hooked her arm in Riley's and walked her out.

"How could he act so calm about it?" Riley asked. "That poor baby girl. It's hard enough to be an orphan."

"I'm sure he'll look into it," Jane soothed. "He said he would." Of course she didn't believe him, but she would look into it, that was for sure. "Let me know if anything else like that comes up, will you?"

"Yes. Absolutely. One hundred percent!" Riley headed off to work in the preschool again, and Jane finally made her way to the bathrooms.

The dorm showers that the men were using was surprisingly clean, if you didn't count the overwhelming odor of body spray that the male youths had left behind. Other than that, it was an easy job. Spray and wipe and a little polish.

The ladies' room was messier, if only because long hair tended to shed and bits of toilet paper and tissue from teenage girls' makeup routines didn't always make it into the garbage can. But, overall, also an easy clean.

Jane had a list of bathrooms that needed their daily cleaning. It was long. She brushed her hair out of her eyes and wished she had her trusty kerchief to tie it back with. And her own cleaning caddy. The next bathrooms were the "everyone" bathrooms outside the dining hall. Single stall toilets that seemed to attract a line before meals. She had low expectations for their cleanliness.

She propped open the first door with her hip and dragged her mop and bottle of all-purpose cleaner in with her. The man sitting on the floor wasn't nearly as embarrassed as she was when she realized the room was occupied.

He wasn't embarrassed at all, in fact.

He was dead.

CHAPTER 6

The body in the bathroom was that of the middle-aged Caucasian man. At least that's what Jane surmised. The gray hair gave him the look of an over-fifty. His skin was pale, his eyes open, startling blue, and very, very dead.

This wasn't her first time at the dead-body rodeo so she sucked in the disgust that toyed with her gut, and examined him. There was no blood. There was also no obvious sign of a struggle: no ripped clothes, holes in the wall or other torn and broken things in the bathroom with him. His hands were not clenched in fists, but were curled loosely. It might just have been because he was dead, but it was possible he had been attempting to make a fist.

The bathroom door had not been locked. Perhaps he had gone in to be sick and then died instead.

He didn't stink, neither like a decomposing body or like barf. It was November, so it wasn't hot enough to make a body decompose fast. Also, the body was stiff with rigor mortis so he couldn't have been dead that long. She patted her cell phone with a shaky hand, ready to call 911, but remembered she was not in

America and had no idea what the protocol in Mexico was when you found a dead body.

While in the bathroom taking stock of the death scene, she had managed to stay cool and controlled. A professional private detective. But when she stepped into the sunny fall day in Baja California, with voices of children playing on the playground and birds singing in trees, she shivered. The contrast was too much. In sympathy with his final illness, she was stricken with the urge to be ill and to collapse, but she had to keep herself together.

If Tory and Chase had brought the drug cartel to the orphanage, her job had just gotten a lot more dangerous.

She ran across the orphanage campus to the main office buildings, her lungs burning and legs shaking and mind swimming. She had come to this country to discover why Tory Trives was working a mission trip, not to stumble over a dead man.

The door to the office building was locked.

"Hello, hello, hello?" she cried out, hoping that Miguel, the staff person she was most comfortable with, was inside.

No one answered.

She turned around and leaned against the hard steel door for support and prayed to God. She was here to prove a kid had reformed herself, not for murder.

Mr. Rodriguez ambled up the path, hands in his pockets, whistling. He looked happy.

How could he be happy?

"Mr. Rodriguez! Please, you've got to come with me."

"Slow down, what's the matter?"

"A horrible thing, really horrible. I'm so sorry. In the bathroom. There's a man, a body, I mean…" She didn't usually ramble like this. Maybe she was too much in character of youth missionary.

"I don't understand. Who is in the bathroom? What happened?"

"Just come with me!" She turned and ran. Fortunately, Dr. Rodriguez kept pace with her.

She pulled open the bathroom door and waved her hands at the body. "See? Here. He's dead. I found him."

Dr. Rodriguez put a comforting hand on her shoulder. "Thank you for coming to me." His voice was low, the happiness gone. He had reverted to the tired old man she had met that morning. "Sit down over there," he turned her to a bench, "and wait. I will take care of everything."

What followed was a rapid fire of sounds and images flashing like gunshots all around her.

Sirens.

Police.

Fast, loud Spanish conversations swirling over her head.

A small man in a dark uniform with a big gun.

An ambulance.

A tense conversation in Ben Rodriguez's office where a translator helped her explain to two policemen how she had found the body.

It was the Twilight Zone version of the body-finding scenarios she had been in before, the fear of corrupt police and cartel retribution making her dizzy.

When it was over, Ben gave her a platonic side hug. "You did okay. Don't worry. That was all routine."

She nodded. "But who was he?"

Ben wiped his eye. "Pat Bromfield, one of our housefathers."

"Oh no!"

Ben sat down at his desk. "He'd been with his family for seven years. Seven years. Those poor kids."

"But he wasn't Mexican."

Ben smiled sadly. "He came on a short term trip and fell in love with one of our local ladies. He and Olivia had been so happy. They married and he stayed on as maintenance. Kept begging to be houseparents. We had so many kids we couldn't say no."

"He spoke Spanish?"

"Very well. He had been a Spanish teacher in L.A. before he came here." He picked up his phone. "If you don't mind, Jane, I have some phone calls to make."

"Of course." She let herself out and ran to find Jake.

"Slow down!" His voice came from behind her. "I've been waiting outside that office door for two hours."

She stopped, panting. "Jake, what's going on at this orphanage?"

"We're going to have to get an insider who likes to talk. You've got two bodies and an abuse case so far."

"Two bodies?"

"You didn't forget the big traditional funeral happening this evening, did you?"

"I wasn't counting that, but maybe I had better." Jane bit her lip. Who was it Miguel had said was dead? A maintenance man?

"And I think you'd better call Flora and find out what she wants you to do."

"Good idea."

Jane locked herself in one of the single stall bathrooms farthest from the hubbub of the orphanage to make her call.

"SCORI, how can I help you?" Flora's assistant answered the phone.

"Miranda, this is Jane. I need Flora immediately."

"Sorry Jane, she's undercover right now."

"What about Rocky?"

"*Nein*. He's golfing with some donors."

"I've got a serious problem in Mexico. Two suspicious deaths."

"No kidding." Miranda didn't sound impressed.

"I came here on a drugs case—one that we are pretty sure isn't real in the first place. Now two dead men. What would Flora want me to do?"

"Take notes."

"Of course, but what else?"

"What else is there? Observe and deduce, Jane."

"Can you have her call me back when she's free? I really want to talk to her."

"She's in deep right now. I have no idea when I will see her or hear from her, but I'll put a Post-it on her desk."

"Gee, thanks."

"Chin up, Jane. You're a real detective now."

Jane hung up. The conversation had not been worth the international charges.

Jake was waiting on the other side of the bathroom door.

"Let's take a walk." She looped her arm through his. "I think we need to talk."

"Yup."

They wandered over to the orchard where they could walk between the almond trees in privacy.

"I have no reason to think that Chase is selling drugs," Jake began. "But something is fishy."

"I can't decide if Tory is using or not. She has the look, and she went missing yesterday, and she actually wanted to clean the bathrooms. But it could still be jet lag and allergies."

"And now this man is dead. Did you learn who he was?" Jake asked.

"Yeah." She repeated the story of the only Anglo house father.

"Two kind of young-for-dying white guys dying of non-violent causes in the same week That's fishier than Chase's fan hangout."

"I want to shadow Tory. I need to find her now, and not let her out of my sight. You never know, this Pat fellow might have seen something he shouldn't have seen."

"Then again," Jake said, "the other fellow died before we got here."

Jane tugged her hair into a tight ponytail. "Sure. If this place is a regular delivery site for drug mules who have a perfectly legal reason to be here, any number of people could have been killed through the years. In fact, Flora warned me that if this was a real drug situation it could get pretty dangerous."

"I'll buddy up to Mr. Ben while you shadow Tory. We might be able to learn the cause of death early that way."

"Okay, babe." She gave his arm a squeeze.

The funeral was canceled. Claude Marshall would stay in the cooler at the funeral home for a little while longer. Nothing had been said about the death of Pat being suspicious, but the volunteers were sequestered in their dorms and all of the resident families met in the Bromfield home to comfort the bereaved. Only Miguel, the volunteer coordinator, and Ginger, the permanent preschool volunteer, stayed with the teams—Ginger in the ladies' dorm and Miguel in the men's.

"What did the body look like?" Riley, the girl who had reported the possible abuse, asked Jane.

Jane described him, leaving out the staring, dead eyes and the body stiff with rigor.

"That was him." Riley's voice was a low, dramatic whisper. "That's the guy that was hitting the little girl."

"I thought you said he was spanking her," Jane clarified.

"Hitting, spanking, same thing."

"No, it's not. You have to be really clear when you talk about things like this."

"He was spanking her really hard, with an open hand, sometimes on her bottom, sometimes on the back of her legs, and a few times on the shoulder. I call that hitting."

"Hmm. That does sound a bit like a gray area." They were huddled on Jane's bunk together, across from Tory's bunk.

Tory was lying down with her eyes closed and her earphones on.

So far Jane had managed to keep an eye on her. Being confined to their dorms had helped. "Can you be sure we are talking about the same guy?"

"Yeah. It was the white dad, in house four."

"Ginger," Jane called out.

Ginger was sitting on the floor with some of the high school girls, having an emotional talk about the fragility of life. She stood up. "Yeah?"

"Got a minute?"

"Sure." Ginger laid a comforting hand on the shoulder of a girl with braided black hair, then joined Jane and Riley.

"I just wanted to know what house the Bromfields live in." Jane patted the bed, inviting Ginger to join them.

"They're in house four." Ginger crouched on the floor in front of them.

"How many kids do they have?"

"Ten, just like everyone."

"That's sure a lot of kids. How do they keep them from fighting?" Riley jumped right into the hot topic, though Jane would have preferred to ease her way in.

Ginger tilted her head. "Depends on the family, but there are some guidelines the families all adhere to. Very cultural. Traditional."

"Rules about things like spanking and so on?" Jane asked.

Ginger frowned. "I heard about the complaint that was made." She gave Riley a stern look. "Annabella is a bully. Yes, little Ezra hit her, but it was after many months of constant abuse. Girls can be bullies, too."

"Of course. Poor Ezra." Jane nodded in sympathy. Girls and boys had equal opportunity to be brats and bullies.

"Pat doesn't—didn't—abuse the kids. He was a great father." Ginger's chin quivered. "He was very creative."

Jane tried to picture the headstand situation.

Creative?

That was one word for it.

Then the picture that the preschool girls had drawn came to mind, and the headstand game in the playground. "Did he come up with the idea for headstands as punishment?" She tried to sound interested and impressed rather than horrified.

"Yes. Such a clever idea. He said he wants them to turn their attitudes around. It's like . . ." She paused to think. "It's like a tangible application of an abstract idea. It helps the kids understand." She nodded vigorously.

Jane nodded, but only to keep Ginger talking. "If the boys and girls are anything like I was, I bet they become very good at headstands."

Ginger shook her head. "Only girls. Men have to be taught to lead. The girls need to learn a spirit of quiet and humility."

Jane swallowed a shudder. Not that she didn't think people in general would improve with a spirit of quiet and humility, but the way that Ginger parroted the response as though it was memorized, and the way that the little boys were called men . . . it made Jane's skin crawl. "Do all of the families follow his . . . creative techniques?"

"Not yet, but he's been meeting with the other dads, praying together, mentoring and stuff. He raised a big family back home before he came here. So he knows his stuff."

Tory sat up, catching Jane's eye. "What time is it?" she asked, with a yawn.

Jane checked her phone. "Nine."

Tory flopped back down again without a word.

"Are Pat's grown up kids still in America?"

"Oh, they're all over. Some are missionaries!" She grinned huge, clearly proud of the Bromfield clan.

"What about their mom?" Jane asked.

Ginger narrowed her eyes. "She left him. That's when he came here. Nursing his broken heart."

"Were you here back then?" Riley wasn't playing Jane's game. Her question was full of disbelief.

"No." Ginger shrugged. "But he gives—gave—his testimony a lot. Pretty much every Friday at chapel with the volunteers."

"Ahh." Riley managed to sound like she knew what was really going on. Jane only wished she had that confidence.

"So sad that you all lost Claude and Pat. That leaves two big, empty holes here at the orphanage." Jane spoke low and smooth, trying to keep Ginger from catching on to Riley's attitude.

Ginger sighed sadly. "It really does. A good father is gone, and a dear laborer. Claude was tireless in his efforts for the kids."

The group of girls she had been talking with spread out to their various bunks, some to read, some to pray, probably some to text boys back home. Ginger rolled a sleeping bag out on an empty bunk. "I'll be staying with you all for the next few nights. Just until they figure things out." She popped earbuds in, her contribution to the evening over.

Riley reverted to a whisper. "It's a culture of abuse, Jane. These poor kids. Mr. Rodriguez won't do anything about it. He's probably part of it."

"I don't like the sound of it either, but let's hold off on making a judgment yet. I think we should talk to some of the housemothers and see what they say first."

"Should we split them up between us?"

Jane gave Riley a quick once over. The young missionary wasn't subtle, that was for sure, but she was motivated, and not already committed to shadowing a shady teen. "I have something else I am supposed to do—its possibly related—do you think you can try and talk to two or three women tomorrow and report back? We'll see if I can talk to the rest after it, but I have to—"

"You have to keep stalking that rock star?" She gave Jane the same kind of look she had given Ginger.

"We've been that obvious?" Jane sucked in her cheeks, disappointed. "I'll tell you all about it but not yet." She wasn't whispering, since whispers carried better than extremely quiet voices.

Riley looked impressed. "We need a secret meeting place tomorrow." Her bright blue eyes were wide with excitement and she quivered like a plucked bow.

"Let me figure it out. I'll tell you the plan during breakfast. In the meantime . . ."

"I'll be cool, and I'll go to bed." She bounced out of Jane's bunk and across the dorm to the side where her team was bunking. as excited as a child on Christmas Eve.

Perhaps Riley was exactly what Jane's investigation needed.

Jane looked over at Tory. Tory was staring at her through narrowed eyes, the cord to her earphones in her hand, not plugged into any kind of device at all.

CHAPTER 7

Jane could only assume that Tory had heard everything. She prayed throughout the night, her fitful sleep good for that at least. She needed to figure out how to smooth the situation over. Should she sit down with Tory and Chase and explain in all honesty? Should she ignore what Tory had heard and keep up her undercover thing? Should she give some half-truths—or half of the whole truth? Somewhere in between?

Her aversion to lying made her want to bare it all, perhaps even to the whole team, but the idea that her boss wouldn't like that nagged at her. At first light she ran to the bathroom, locked herself in and called Flora. For once, Flora answered.

"Listen, I've got a problem." Jane laid out the situation with the dead body and Tory hearing the conversation.

For a moment, Flora was silent. "I was sure hoping this wasn't a drug cartel kind of job. If I had had any reason for concern, I wouldn't have sent you. Rocky and I would have gone." Her voice held a tone of disappointment. Whether from putting a new detective in danger or from missing the adventure, Jane wasn't sure.

"But what do I do about Tory?"

"Your instincts are good, if a bit extreme. No need to sit the whole team down, since you've been dying to go into missionary work your whole life, but it's time to talk to Tory like an adult. You and Jake and Chase and Tory need to find some alone time and discuss the job her father hired you for."

The idea repulsed Jane, even though she had also thought of it. It tasted too much like failure. "Are you sure? We were really starting to get somewhere."

"You called me for my experience and wisdom, right?"

"Yes."

"Then don't talk back. I'm old enough to be your grandmother, and I have seen a few things in life. Get them alone as soon as you can."

Jane scratched her head. Alone would be hard considering the situation. "And if I can't?"

"Then you have a hostile teenager possibly selling drugs, and probably also have a murderer on the loose. I would personally not let 'can't' be an option."

"Yes, of course." Jane sent up a quickie prayer to that end. "Flora, I'm not sure what I am doing here."

"You're finding out what Tory and Chase are up to, and you are about to sit down and ask them directly. We don't mess around with murderers."

"Okay. I can do that."

"I'll be praying for you. Rocky can be there in two days, if you need him. If things feel out of your control, tell me. This case has a big expense account. Mr. Trives would do anything for his daughter."

"Thank you. I'll keep in touch." Jane took a deep breath and squared her shoulders. She did *not* need Rocky Wilson to come rescue her.

The director of the orphanage and his wife came personally to let the volunteers out of the dorms. Nadine, the director's wife, was a lovely woman with a shiny silver streak in her hair. Her big blue eyes were shadowed with sadness, but her warm smile seemed to offer that motherly comfort that everyone wanted. She reached her hands out to the ladies in their dorm. "We are so sorry that your visit with us has been touched with tragedy, but also so glad that if we have to go through this, we have such a kind, international family of God to grieve with us. Come, let's have breakfast together." Something about her words felt like a benediction and a state speech and welcome all at the same time. The girls seemed to rush forward, like children to their own mother, and followed her into the cafeteria.

Jane hung back and counted heads, making sure she didn't lose track of Tory or Ginger or Riley.

There seemed to be no tension between Jake and Chase as they entered the cafeteria together, but they took seats at opposite ends of the room. Jane settled herself next to her husband.

He leaned in to kiss her neck and whisper sweet nothings.

Jane responded to his affection with a conspiratorial whisper."We have to get Tory and Chase alone. She's onto us."

Jake groaned, low in his throat, "Have I ever told you how hot it is to be married to a detective?"

She blushed and scooted away a bit.

He leaned in one more time. "Nab Tory after breakfast and drag her behind the preschool. I'll meet you there with Chase."

Jane nodded and filled her plate with scrambled eggs, beans, and a few orange slices. Nab Tory? Easier said than done, but she'd try.

"*Buenos días*." Miguel took his place at the front of the room. "I don't have job assignments today, but I do have directions. The *policia* are still doing interviews and working in the area. I do not know where the investigation stands and cannot answer any question about it. I can tell you that there are three places you are welcome to be until they give us more information: the volunteer lounge, the cafeteria, and the chapel. We will do our best to communicate with you all clearly and quickly, but . . ." He looked around slowly, making eye contact with many of the people, and took a deep breath. "I want you all to keep your papers on you at all times. Do not release them to anyone. Not the police, not staff. We have photo copies of all of your entrance documents in our safe. Your team leaders have photo copies in their possession. If anyone needs to see anything, they can see our copies. Please take this seriously. Do not give up your papers. If someone demands it, refer them to staff." He cleared his throat. "This is a new situation for us. We have not faced anything like this before. It is of extreme importance that you do not go alone anywhere right now. Limit yourselves to the bathrooms attached to the three spaces the police have okayed for your use. Don't go to your dorms until we get the all clear. Don't go from room to room alone." He looked from table to table, then gave a weak smile. "If nothing else, you will have stories to tell for the rest of your lives." On that note, he got up and left. No questions, no prayer.

He seemed, frankly, terrified.

Jake stayed close to Jane in the line to bus their plates. "Trust me. We need to meet behind the preschool. Don't freak out."

"Of course not." Sometimes she was opposed to lying, and sometimes she lied through her teeth. The police said there were three places they were allowed to be and grassy patch behind the preschool was not one of them.

"Tory. Hey, Tory," Jane called from behind. Tory had been avoiding Jane all morning.

Tory turned, a frown on her face.

"Wait up."

Tory gripped Chase's arm, but stood still.

"Can you come with me, for just a second? I have something I need to explain," she said as soon as she was in whispering distance.

Tory turned to Chase, her brow furrowed.

Chase shrugged.

"Fine." The one word came from between Tory's gritted teeth.

Tory's body language reflected exactly what Jane was feeling as they scuttled to their designated spot. Shoulders high, head constantly flicking glances backwards to see if anyone was watching them. Steps stiff, but fast. Scared was a good word for the look. Terrified was the actual feeling.

The two women leaned against the wall of the preschool, catching their breath. Jake stood guard at the corner of the building, one eye out for *policia*. Chase locked his hands behind his back and paced.

Tory turned to Jane. "I'm not stupid. My father hired you to babysit me because he hates Chase."

"That's not exactly it," Jane interjected.

"Oh no? Are you saying my father didn't hire you? Are you claiming you being here has nothing at all to do with how my father feels about me dating an older guy who's in a band?"

Jane was silent.

"Exactly. But now there has been a murder, and since you are in my dad's pay, you're going to try and get Chase locked up in a Mexican prison so I never see him again." Her face was red with anger.

Chase stopped in front of Jane, his shoulders squared, his formidable head forward. "What's your game?"

"Mr. Trives hired a private detective to follow you and find out if you came to Mexico to deal drugs. I'm the detective. I'm supposed to come up either with evidence that you are dealing drugs or that you aren't. It's impossible to prove a negative, so if you aren't dealing drugs, we're all in trouble. And if you are dealing drugs, I guess just the two of you are in trouble. I work for the Senior Corps of Retired Investigators and am serving my apprenticeship. Things have come to a head with this murder, but only because I foolishly exposed my position to Tory. If you want to explain what you're doing here, you'll make all of our lives easier."

"We, unlike you, are here to serve the needy," Tory spit out with venom. "Only one thing in this world is more disgusting than hypocrisy and lies, and that is working for my father. Come on, Chase."

Chase stood his ground. "How do we know what you are saying is true?"

"Does that sound like a lie?" Jake asked with a sarcastic laugh. "She told you who she works for and what she was hired to do."

"We don't need to tell these two anything." Tory tugged on Chase's sleeve., the slight difference in their age apparent by the way he gently patted her hand to calm her down.

"I'm not selling drugs. I'm serving the needy, just like everyone else. Come on, Tory, we don't want to get caught in no man's land."

Tory shot Jane a bitter look and turned on her heel. They left fast, and holding hands.

"That went well." Jake didn't sound sarcastic.

"In whose world?"

"I believe him."

"Yeah, me too. He's not selling drugs. They're doing something they consider good, but it's also not the orphanage work."

"Exactly. So we can leave it. Let's go back to the cafeteria, have a cup of coffee, and wait around until they let us get back to work." He yawned. "I don't know about you, but I've had a week of hard labor so far, and don't mind a break."

Jane went with him, also aware that it wasn't a good idea to linger in places the *policía* had declared off limits. "The trouble is I've been hired for a job. If I could find out what they are doing here, under the cover of the orphanage, I could prove they aren't buying, or selling, or transporting drugs."

"And you'd also like to solve the murder."

"It would be nice."

"And then I could introduce you as 'my wife Jane, international crime-fighter.'"

Jane laughed. "I like the sound of that." They paused at the door into the cafeteria. "I'm not going to let up, just so you know."

"It was an empty hope, and a momentary lapse on my part. You fight the good fight. I'm going to caffeinate myself."

The cafeteria was mostly empty, as the volunteers had preferred the more comfortable seating in the lounge, or perhaps the spiritual comfort of the chapel. Jake filled paper cups of tepid coffee for himself and Jane and then settled at a table with three members of the other volunteer team.

"This has all been kind of weird, right?"

Two blonde girls nodded.

"I never expected this," a young man with small hoop earrings in both ears said. "I've been to Mexico for short-term trips five times now and never had a murder investigation."

"Do you think it really was murder?" Jane asked in a hushed voice.

"They wouldn't still have us under lock and key if it was, like, a heart attack or something," the earring kid said.

"Besides, he was perfectly healthy. I saw him playing with the kids," one of the blondes said.

"Where?" Jane jumped in a little too aggressively with her question, and regretted it. She softened her tone. "I mean, like, was he running around or something? How do you know it meant he was healthy?"

"I was washing windows and I was at his picture window. He was playing with his little ones, teaching them to do headstands."

"Aw." Jane swallowed revulsion. Was he constantly punishing the poor kids? How could this girl see that and think they were playing? "They had a happy memory as the last of their daddy . . ."

She scrunched up her face. "I guess."

"Tell her the truth, Pen," the other blonde girl said. "You saw them playing, but the little girl was bawling, and the older brother was laughing at her, and then the dad got all mad."

"Well . . . sure, but it was kind of normal. You know how it is, right?" She looked to Jake for confirmation. "When you are fighting and your dad gets fed up?"

Jake nodded. "My dad to a T. How mad did this guy get? Mine used to find a paddle. Never used it, but always wacked it against the palm of his hand, threatening us."

"Yes! Exactly. He took off his belt and did that, like he was going to whip them. My dad did that once. Scared me to death. I cried for fifteen minutes afterwards, and he didn't even spank me."

"Did Pat spank the boy for teasing his sister?"

"I don't know. It looked kind of . . . private. So I moved on to the other window. I mean, family time is tough, isn't it? I'd have hated to have people watching in the window when I was getting punished."

"Can't blame you at all." Jake took a swig of his coffee.

"But he seemed healthy and energetic, huh?" Jane asked. "That does seem bad. If he had been all red faced, and huffing and puffing like my dad before his heart attack..." One lie seemed to follow the other. Her dad was, and had always been, the picture of health.

"That's why I remembered it so clearly," Pen said. "Because he hadn't been out of control or red faced or anything like a person about to have a heart attack would be. He was mad, but looked fine."

"Even Jane gets red faced when she's mad at me." Jake chuckled.

As if by command, Jane blushed. "Jake!"

"See?"

Pen looked closely at Jane. "You know, he was a little red faced. So . . . maybe . . . I don't know."

"Maybe you don't know anything." The earring guy spoke again. "Just because you saw him before he died doesn't mean you are suddenly an important witness." He looked disgusted with her.

"And Dad never took his belt off to spank you. You make him sound like a monster." Ahh. Sibling. That explained his disgust.

"He did too, and I don't know why you don't remember it. You caused the whole thing."

Their conversation deteriorated into an argument about some event from least ten years in the past.

Jane sipped her coffee and wondered if the cops had thought to ask the volunteers what they had seen. Perhaps she could get an upper hand on the investigation. She'd just need to find someone who had seen Pat Bromfield more immediately before he had died.

Though she wandered from cafeteria to chapel to volunteer lounge, chatting with everyone she could, Jane found no one who had seen Pat shortly before she had found his body. Or at least no one willing to admit it.

She gave up on that quest—for the time being—and settled into a threadbare recliner with her Bible hoping to find a little solace in the Good Word. It wouldn't have the solution to the crime in it, but it was better than dwelling on her failures as she tried to come up with her next move.

She was humming along to the forty-second Psalm when Jake joined her. "I've just been with the police. They interviewed me. I don't know why they took so long seeing as how I'm married to the girl who found the body." He frowned dramatically. "I like to be a bit more important than that."

Jane closed her Bible. "How did it go? Did you learn anything?"

"It went very well, and yes I did. By inference at least. The questions they asked me were interesting. Did I have access to the house Pat lived in? No more access than any other volunteer. But as I had been assigned to construction all week, you might even say I had less access than most."

"Seems like a weird way to start the interview." It seemed to Jane, at least, that that kind of information was easily obtainable by the work schedule.

"It did catch me by surprise. That's for sure. Next they asked if I had a medical background, which I don't. I've never been more glad to not be a doctor."

"That's also kind of weird question." Jane was hoping she'd be able to build a picture from the clues Jake was dropping, but the first two didn't match at all.

"I agree. They also asked a bunch of normal questions, but the question that led me to my genius moment, the inference of inferences, was if I knew how Pat's heart medicine had ended up in the men's dorm."

"That's kind of a big reveal." Jane laughed, the result of nerves and surprise. "If I were you I would have led with that just now."

"No way, that's the kind of thing you build up to."

Jane frowned. "But why you?"

"Ah, well, that's the next big deal. It turns out Bromfield is—was—on the board of directors of Escape International."

Jane sucked in a breath. "So he's technically your boss?"

"Kind of. Escape has a big board. Bromfield has lived in Mexico longer than I've been on staff, so I've never met him and didn't even recognize his name. That said, of course the board does have the power to fire me from my position as a development officer, but they wouldn't because I rock. It's a coincidence, but not a big one considering."

"Considering what?"

"Considering Escape is Southern California based, Pat has had a long history of work in Evangelical non-profits in California, and that the world of mission work is a little on the small side. But it was enough of a coincidence for them to question me closely about the heart medicine of a man who died mysteriously in Mexico while I happened to be in town."

"This seems, on the surface, to be the stuff of nightmares."

"Nah. They were reasonable men. They seemed to understand that I have about twenty bosses and that this one who I had never met and didn't know had very little power over me personally. They also seemed to recognize that I wouldn't have known he was on heart medicine, and wouldn't have had a way to sneak it out of his bathroom."

"And now we know how he died."

"Now we can infer that he died by failing to take his heart medicine. And we can infer that someone snuck it away from him."

"If he had known it was missing he would have just gotten more," Jane mused. "So the killer must have substituted his pills for some that looked the same."

"Another good inference." Jake stood up. "I think we can't make any more of it than that though."

"But what about the pills being in your dorm?"

"It's been several days and they didn't find them the first day, so I think someone recently put them as far away from themselves as they could."

"Another good inference."

"True, but it only supports what the other facts seem to indicate. Someone with access and knowledge wanted Bromfield dead, was willing to wait for it, and wanted it to be untraceable."

"If they wanted it to be untraceable, why didn't they flush his pills? Or even better, why didn't they just put them back after he died? Then no one would know."

Jake sat quietly for a moment. "Maybe the autopsy revealed he hadn't been taking them."

"Okay. I can go with that. Perhaps something in the autopsy revealed he hadn't taken his pills. We don't know what the pills were, or how they worked, so we can only guess that was possible. The killer had replaced the fakes with the real ones, flushing the fakes and flushing the correct number of pills that Bromfield was supposed to have taken. But they get word that the police know the truth and they have to get rid of the right pills."

"Why?" Jake leaned close, forehead to forehead with Jane.

"Because . . . access to the pills is limited enough to shed light on the killer, and she—probably his wife—had to make her attempt at a cover up disappear. And she ditched them in the volunteer dorm to throw suspicion on someone else—anyone else at all, really. Your connection with Bromfield, thin as it is, is an unfortunate coincidence that was actually very useful to us."

"Not bad. I could be convinced of that if I was on a jury and you had some physical proof."

"Which is one of the many things we don't and won't have."

"Find out what permanent staff or residents have been near the men's dorm lately. That's a start."

"You're a genius, and I love you." Jane gave him a big long kiss to thank him for the first real break she had had since coming to Mexico, and also because she was missing him at night.

CHAPTER 8

A chill wind blew across the field as she walked to the chapel. November in Northern Baja wasn't an equatorial paradise. They had finally received permission to hold Claude Marshall's funeral. But it would be doubly sad since the families and full-time staff would essentially be mourning both men.

Jake nabbed Jane before she entered the chapel. "Everyone will be in there."

Jane nodded, not feeling like the obvious deserved a huge kind of response.

"Everyone. The whole staff, all of the families. Even the police seem to be inside, watching so that no one could slip out, I guess. The whole orphanage will be abandoned."

Jane froze. Her face lit up. A shiver of excitement ran down her spine. "Of course." They slipped to the side of the chapel with no windows.

"We can watch from here. When the last of the slowpokes enter the chapel, this whole place is at our disposal."

They didn't have an attendance list to check off, but after twenty minutes, no one else walked up to the chapel door, and the police were still largely absent from the courtyard.

"While they could probably see us, they also probably aren't looking," Jane said.

Jake just nodded. "House four first, yes?"

"Definitely." They headed to the Bromfield house, sneaking the long way around the buildings, just in case. It was unlocked, and they let themselves right in. "Good thing the cops asked us about our access to the house before we did this. Make sure you are careful with your fingerprints." Jane wasn't nearly as cavalier about Jake's connection to the dead man as he was, and the idea of him sneaking around while under suspicion hit her like a rock, just as they walked in.

But she pushed the fear aside, and went straight to the master bedroom.

The whole house was painted concrete, with linoleum floors, easy to keep cool, inexpensive to build. Woven throw rugs gave it a homey air. The furniture in the bedroom had the cast-off look one would expect of a place run entirely on American donations. A huge dresser of solid wood from the 1970s paired with a bed that had no headboard.

She pulled open the drawers of the dresser. The top held ladies' clothes, the next men's. She skipped the mother's drawers and dug through Pat's clothes. One pair of khakis, three pairs of jeans, at least five pairs of cargo shorts. But all of them with empty pockets. An assortment of polo shirts, worn thin with age.

The last of the five drawers didn't have any clothes in it. Just one of those jumbles of string that the woman had told her were "cultural." Jane picked it up and ran her fingers through it. The strings were all the same unbleached color, and most of them had a series of knots, though Jane couldn't figure out the pattern. Though she would have loved to take serious time to study it, she put it back and moved to the closet.

One church dress, one pair of sandals. Nothing else. If Pat had had a nice suit and dress shoes, they were probably waiting for him at the funeral home. If and when the morgue released him, they would dress him in his nicest clothes.

Jake poked his head in the door. "Anything in here?"

"Not yet." Jane knelt by the bed and looked under it, but it was empty. Not even extra blankets or dust bunnies.

She joined Jake in the living room. "You find anything?" Their voices were whispers, their words spare, and their motions jerky and slow, desperate to not be noticed though there was only one window, and it faced the empty courtyard.

"Just this." He pointed to a chart on the wall. Ten Spanish names down one side. A series of words across the top: *limpiar ropa, lava platos*—regular chores, also in Spanish. Boxes with stars, some with check marks. "What do you think that means?" She pointed to whole row of black squares next to Annabella's name.

"Discipline, I guess."

Jane traced the line of squares with her fingers. "Check the kids' rooms?"

Jake nodded.

Jane went to the girls' room. Two bunk beds and one single bed on a simple frame. Two medium dressers. This room wasn't as empty feeling as the parents' though. The beds had cheerful blankets. One top bunk had a bright, clean baby doll, carefully swaddled. Two of them had matching teddy bears. The single bed had a book, open on the pillow. A laundry basket against the wall spilled over with small dolls, stuffed animals, and plastic toys.

Jane opened one of the dresser drawers. The girls' clothes were folded and stacked nicely, except for the drawer full of tights and underpants, but as Jane well knew, it was almost impossible to keep that drawer tidy.

The closet was the same. A smattering of church clothes and shoes. Not enough for five American little girls, but plenty if each of these girls only wore one dress a week. And five school uniforms carefully hung. It seemed a pity each girl only had one uniform, but perhaps they had two and were wearing the other set. Still, nothing fishy. Nothing that screamed "my daddy beats me." Everything looked fine.

"The boys' room is perfectly normal," Jake said, when she met him in the living room again.

"As is the girls'. Not even weirdly over-normal. Just actually normal." The chore chart with the black squares made Jane sad. A tiny window into a life of weird rules and borderline abuse, but no evidence. Nothing you could use to call attention to it, to say "this isn't okay."

Jake shrugged, clearly as disappointed as Jane felt.

They checked the bathroom, with careful attention to the medicine cabinet. But all they found was enough toilet paper for a family of twelve, two toothbrush holders packed full, and toothpaste. Whatever the heart medicine situation had been, it was clearly in an evidence baggy with the police. There was no sign of it in the bathroom or bedroom.

Next they upended the living room, but put it back together again with care. Nothing tucked under cushions or furniture. Nothing hiding in the cupboards in the kitchen. "My mind keeps going back to that cultural craft project," Jane said, as they shut the door to house four.

"The string thing you were telling me about?"

"It's the only thing that stands out, don't you think?"

"Sure, but how do you get someone to tell you what it means?"

"Good question." She mulled over ideas. "After the funeral we need to hang out in the teen house."

Jake raised an eyebrow.

"Trust me."

Two sets of parents were entrusted with raising the teenagers—one for the girls, and one for the boys. When the girls and boys hit fourteen they moved into the teen houses, a dorm-style living arrangement, and stayed there until high school was over. It sounded miserable, to Jane, but then, there had to be a way to make room for new children in each family if you wanted to run a family-style orphanage.

It wasn't until the next day that Jane and Jake were able to hang out with the teenagers, and at that it was getting late. Their two-week mission trip was more than half over. The police hadn't told them they couldn't leave the country, but that might change when their flights actually came up. They were allowed back in the dorms, but otherwise required to limit their movements to a few buildings. While the teen homes weren't on the acceptable list of places for volunteers to hang out, Jane and Jake needed to risk it.

This time, instead of sneaking around behind buildings when no one was looking, they decided to go for confidence as a cover and walked boldly across the courtyard together, from the cafeteria to the teen houses, which stood next to each other.

No one stopped them.

They split up again, Jane to the girls and Jake to the boys.

It was the siesta hour on a Saturday and five of the twelve girls who currently lived in the dorm were lounging in a family room.

Jane joined them.

One girl, with deep dimples in her round face, smiled at Jane.

"How are you guys holding up?" Jane sat on the overstuffed couch next to the dimpled girl.

"Not so well." Her English was very smooth. "Pat was my house daddy." Her eyes were big, and her lashes long. A good enough reason, in Jane's mind, to keep the boys in their own dorm.

"I'm so sorry. He seems like he was a really good daddy." Jane lied through her teeth, but for a good cause.

The girl nodded. "The only daddy I ever had."

Another girl, sitting across the room, snorted.

"Shut up, Esperanza." Dimples frowned.

"*No quiero.*" Esperanza leaned forward. "Pat was terrible." Her English was heavily accented, but not at all hesitant. Very beautiful and smooth, in fact.

As much as Jane wanted to hear how awful and abusive Pat had been—mostly from a sense of justice, as his death had made the issue moot—she needed to be able to steer the conversation to those string things, and getting the girls in a fight wouldn't help.

"Did you live with them, too?" Jane asked.

"No way. You couldn't have paid me to live there."

The girl with dimples sighed. "He wasn't always like that, though. Not when I lived there."

"What changed?" Jane had to follow up, even though it was still out of the way of her goal. Though he couldn't be held accountable for the possible abuse, it surely had something to do with his death.

"*Este libro.*" Esperanza threw a book on the floor. "It has ruined everything." She looked like she wanted to spit on the book.

"It's not a good book," Dimples acknowledged.

"May I?" Jane picked it up. The book was a comb-bound with a thin card stock cover like a church ladies cook book. It was in Spanish, but the title was simple enough to translate—*God's Way for Girls and Boys.*

"Is this where the headstand thing come from?" Jane asked.

Dimples shuddered. "I don't like it. It's not okay. But when I was six they still spanked us, so what is worse? Trends come and go."

"My father never spanked us," Esperanza said. "And he destroys every copy of this book he can find."

"Who's your father?" Jane leaned forward, excited by the unexpected revelations. Maybe this man was a vigilante who had killed the abusive father.

"Jorge Estevez." She looked at the floor. "He moved away last year."

"Ahh." Jane sat back. So not this week's murderer . . . probably. "Where did he go?"

"My parents moved to the new orphanage we are opening in Oaxaca. I'm going to work there when I graduate." She looked up, a hopeful light in her hazel eyes.

Jane smiled at her. "They don't approve of this new discipline method?"

"No. They were born in . . . in . . . the twentieth *siglo*. They are not . . . mmm . . . *ancianos*." She shrugged, her English failing.

"Modern parents."

"*Sí*. Exactly. Perfect parents."

"My parents were perfect, too," Dimples said.

"Perfectly horrible."

The other girls had been ignoring the argument until this, but one of them looked up from a book and threw a pillow at Esperanza. "*Nadie es perfecto*." Nobody is perfect.

"What do you guys usually do on the weekend?" Jane had to turn the conversation before it exploded.

"This," the girl who threw the pillow said. "Sometimes you *Americanos* come hang out with us, sometimes not. What do you do?"

"I like to knit." It was a lie, but it was in a good cause.

Pillow-thrower frowned. "What is knit?"

"With yarn? String?" Jane made the motions with her hands . . . sort of. She purposefully made it look as much like what the house mother had been doing with the strings as she could.

"*Como las madres*?" Pillow-thrower directed her question to Esperanza, who appeared to be the oldest of the girls.

"Like tying them?" Esperanza asked.

"Sort of." Jane nodded. "Do any of you do that? Or your mothers?"

Pillow-thrower stood up and nudged a girl who had been sitting at her feet. "*Venga, Mami.*" The two girls left the room.

Dimples bit her lip. "I don't."

Esperanza laughed. "Of course not, Maria. You aren't old enough yet." Esperanza's posture improved, her shoulders straightened. "Eva is teaching me. Very interesting work."

"Very cultural?" Jane asked.

"*Exactamente*. Very cultural. Making stories in string. Keeping records with knots. Very cultural, very beautiful."

"Ahh, I think that is a little different than what I do. Can you tell me about it?"

Dimples shook her head, subtly.

Esperanza smirked. "It is only for women. The men don't understand it. It is like...our language. A way we can . . ." She scratched her head. "A way we can tell our stories and yet be safe."

"Do you have many stories that would put you in danger?" Jane tried to control her nerves, but she had difficulty, so she tucked her shaking hands under her legs.

"No, no." Esperanza laughed. "It is of the past, *si*? From before. Now we just do it to . . . remember."

"*No es de México.*" A girl who had been quietly reading in a glider rocker on the other side of the room frowned.

"It's not Mexican?" Jane asked.

"It's older. Ancient," Esperanza said. "Maybe Peru? But it is good to learn, and who knows, maybe we are *de Peru* also? Orphans have no history." She crossed her arms and sat back, satisfied.

The glider rocker girl let off a long monologue in fast, quiet Spanish that Jane couldn't follow at all.

Dimples responded in English. "Esperanza shouldn't have said anything about it, but it will be okay." She looked at Jane. "This is not for men, or visitors. At an orphanage, where people come and go and never come back, where we kids are a . . . tourist thing . . . we need something that is just for us."

"Ah. I'm sorry. I won't ask any more questions about it."

Esperanza frowned. "Secrets are not safe. When I am in charge someday I won't let there be any secrets at the orphanage."

The girl with the dimples didn't acknowledge Esperanza, and left.

The girl in the glider rocker resumed her reading.

Esperanza looked at the book in Jane's hands. "Keep it. Read it. And make sure no one in your church reads it. For the kids." She got up and left, too.

Jane tucked the book under her arm and went back to her dorm to read. She'd need her Spanish-English dictionary if she wanted to really understand what it was about, but from the conversation she had just had, it seemed well worth understanding.

CHAPTER 9

The book seemed to espouse a minority opinion that women were less than men because Eve had caused the Fall, and that their purpose and role was to forever be apologizing to men for it. At least that was what Jane gathered.

The family discipline was highly biased against girls; family roles were highly biased against women.

It was an ugly book.

She tucked it into her pillowcase and went to the chapel, hoping to find Jake.

He was there, and alone. Jane caught him up with her news on the book, the strings and knots, and everything else she had learned from the girls.

"Interesting." He sat close to her on one of the wooden pews, his hand wrapped around hers. "The boys tell a similar story. Of the seven families, three have been swept up in the philosophies of the book, and the boys that have graduated out of those homes are very mad about it. They do not approve of their sisters being blamed for all of the problems in the homes. They were really clear about it, in fact, going so far to call it out as abuse and a sin."

"Wow." Jane gave a silent prayer of gratitude for the wisdom of the young men. "So they haven't been brainwashed by it."

"Nope, but it looks like the little boys are eating it up."

"Of course they are, little kings in their own houses," Jane said.

"The teen guys aren't having it. They have taken to their own kind of justice."

"So, they beat their little brothers up a bit?"

"I don't know how far they take it, but the amount of anger I heard got under my skin. They sound like they are overcorrecting. I wouldn't be surprised to hear they had really hurt some of these little guys." Jake sounded depressed, which caught his wife off guard.

"Or maybe killed the father who had introduced the idea to the orphanage." Jane spoke low, the implications that the children, supposed to be in a safe place where they could flourish and learn about the Lord, turning to murder was horrific.

Jake was silent, one vein in his temple throbbing, his jaw twitching.

"If they had done it, would their mothers and sisters cover for them? Could this have been a whole community-inspired uprising?" Jane asked.

"What if it was?"

"What if that is the secret being communicated in those bundles of string?" Jane gripped Jake's hand. "If so, they will never report it to the police."

Jake furrowed his brow. "Then again, the widow and the other two women who support this philosophy probably also know the secret knot code, right? It doesn't seem like they could plot to murder someone's husband using a secret code the women are all in on."

"Maybe they have a secret set of secret code strings that she never saw." Jane was quiet. The reality that a good work could be undermined so thoroughly by bad teaching was hard to swallow. It wasn't how she wanted the adult world to work.

"That could be. And anyway, if the heart medicine theory is right, his widow had to be in on it."

"Do you think any of this could have anything to do at all with Chase and Tory?" Jane brought the issue back around to her job. "They're hiding something, and the murder happened now, not last month or next month. Could they have been the assassins? Did they bring a poison to Mexico and use it to kill this guy?"

"How would they have known him? Tory is an Oregon girl and Chase is a Midwest boy. Pat Bromfield was a Southern Californian living in Mexico."

"Don't forget that Chase's little sister came from this orphanage."

Jake stood up and began to pace up and down the middle aisle. "I had forgotten. Sorry. So they do have strong ties, and maybe a reason to dislike the turn things have taken here."

Jane was on the edge of her pew. "Yes. Then again, Chase said his sister hasn't kept in touch with the orphanage at all, and this was his own first visit, so how would they know about a subtle cultural shift like this?" She sat back again and crossed her arms, chewing on the problem.

"He told us that he had never been here and that his sister hadn't kept in touch. But don't you remember how smooth and polished the conversation had been? Like a professional interview. He knew what he was going to say when asked, and he said it."

"So he lied." Jane stated it as fact.

"Or he only told as much as he felt necessary."

"I disagree. If he had been keeping in touch and knew about what you called a weird cultural shift, then saying he didn't have connections was a lie."

"Okay, let's go with he lied." Jake gave in.

"He also lied about meeting fans."

"What if he didn't?"

"Don't be naïve. That was a lie. He's lied twice to us now. Do you think he's one of those musicians who signed with a Christian label just to get famous?" Jane was disgusted by this version of Chase, and hoped it wasn't true. But what were the alternatives?

"No comment."

"You can't no comment at this juncture. You must comment. One thing in my life with you I have always been able to count on has been your comments."

He remained silent.

"Please comment." She gave him a come hither look.

Jake stopped pacing for a moment and faced her. "Remember the midwives at the beginning of Exodus? They told the authorities that the Hebrew babies came too fast so they couldn't drown them."

"They lied to save the babies." Jane reflected.

"Chase and Tory suspected us all along. To them we are paid spies lying about *our* faith on a mission trip. If they are on some kind of crusade they could justify telling us whatever they wanted to satisfy us."

"We're Pharaoh's thugs."

"And her dad is the Pharaoh," Jake agreed.

"But what does Mr. Trives have to do with all of this?" Jane dragged her hands through her hair. As usual, Jake's commentary had been both enlightening and bewildering.

"That's probably one step too far. I don't think he would have hired us to catch Chase in a crime if he was the man secretly behind the crime."

"Or would he?" Jane shook her head, as though sort her thoughts out. "Nah. He wouldn't."

"We're back to square one," Jake said.

"What on Earth is Tory Trives doing at an orphanage in Mexico?" Jane leaned back in her pew and closed her eyes. She needed miraculous intervention, and she needed it in the five days before her plane left for Portland.

As if on cue, but not at all Jane's idea of a miracle, Riley swept into the room and dropped to the floor at Jane's feet. "We need to talk somewhere private."

Jane sat up "It's just me and Jake in here."

Riley looked from side to side eyeing the open windows. "More private than this."

"We're completely alone." Jake sounded impatient.

"I just need Jane for a few minutes. Come with me." Riley jumped up again, not looking to see if Jane followed, and led her across the campus to a small pantry at the back of the cafeteria.

"There are more people around, which means it's louder, which means we're less likely to be overheard. Plus, tucked away in here, no one can read my lips. I didn't like the looks of all of those open windows. People could be hiding just on the other side, listening to anything. Or they could have come in at any minute." She grinned with pride.

"Good idea." Jane had to give her props, it had been good thinking. It irked Jane some that these ideas didn't pop into her head, too. She was the professional, after all.

"I've spoken with five of the housemothers. Not one of them is pro-Bromfield."

"How did you manage this?" Jane sat on a crate of potatoes, ready for a long conversation.

Riley sat on the concrete floor. "I just went from house to house and asked them if I could do anything for them. I meant it, so it was all good. And the police didn't care. Lots of them saw me, but I don't think we're in the kind of danger that Miguel made it sound like."

"Please don't take any dangerous risks, Riley. I would never forgive myself if something happened to you."

Riley waved away Jane's concern. "I was totally fine. But here's the thing. Some of the mothers were cool, but didn't need anything, and weren't in a chatty mood. But five of them were really easy to get into conversation. While they were definitely showing signs of grief—bloodshot eyes from crying and that kind of thing—none of them said that Pat was a friend. And three of them said it was for the best, for the kids."

"That's wild. Are you sure that's how they said it?"

"Oh yes, I'm fluent in Spanish. Went to an immersion school in L.A. before I moved to Kelseyville. That's what they said and that's what they meant."

"Did they elaborate? Explain why, or anything?"

"Maria Paloma Hernandez-Vega from house three did. She was the Bromfields' next door neighbor. It took a few minutes for her to warm up, but once she did—WHOO-boy! She called him, well, in English it would be a misogynist. She said he wasn't even a Christian, not a real one, but a power-hungry man. She said his book disgusted her, and that her dear friend Olivia had changed after her marriage. Had turned from a fun, happy girl to a sad, quiet old person."

"Maria Paloma thought Pat was abusing his wife." Jane stated it, disgusted that her worst fears were probably true.

"Yes. That's what she thinks. And she thinks he was abusive to the kids, but sneaky, though I guess most abusers are. Never hit them in the face, or anywhere a bruise would show. Used humiliation instead of violence. Nothing dirty, of course. Just power hungry. And always the little girls were punished and the little boys

97

were rewarded. This, of course, is what Maria-Paloma said. The other two women who weren't pro-Pat didn't give nearly the same amount of details. They were certain, though, that the death was God's will, and that God knew what he was doing. But Maria Paloma . . . she had a lot to say." Riley's voice got louder as she spoke, and she bounced on her heels. "What can I do now?"

"You've done great, but you scare me. Seriously. If someone killed Pat, I don't want you running around alone."

"Phooey. No one would hurt me. No reason to. I'm just some flighty California girl trying to help the sad people. I'm playing innocent and stupid. It always works."

"I bet." Jane smiled. Riley wasn't that much younger— maybe five years—but she was so happy and optimistic and excitable. Like a puppy. It was the first time Jane had seen what she probably looked like to her mentors, and it wasn't flattering. Youth and enthusiasm were fine in their place, but a bit overwhelming when adults had work to do.

On the other hand, Riley had done a great job and had gotten farther than Jane felt like she had, in a much shorter time. She couldn't fault her for that. Enthusiasm went a long way.

"Okay, you got away with it this time, but if you were to get arrested, or get yourself in the eye of the killer, you'd be in trouble I couldn't help you out of. So listen carefully, and follow directions, okay?"

Riley nodded, face flushed.

"There is a teenage girl named Esperanza, who lives in the girls' teen house. Make friends with her. I've already asked too much about a certain thing they want to keep secret. But Esperanza hates both Pat Bromfield and secrets. So see if you can crack her on the code of the strings."

"The code of the strings?" Riley showed enough sense to repeat the phrase with some disbelief. "That can't be real."

"It is, and I think it holds the key to the killer." Jane gave her voice a dramatic hush. If she could keep Riley engaged with Esperanza she'd keep the kid safe, and maybe even get the information she needed.

"You think Esperanza will spill to me?"

"I don't know. You'll just have to try and find out."

"You've got it." The gleam in Riley's eye was something to behold. Jane wondered if yet another future missionary was being led away by the siren song of investigation.

CHAPTER 10

Jane recognized great gaps in her store of information as she ran through the things she had learned, discovered, or inferred. And one bit related directly to Tory, who had to be her main concern, in the end.

Did Tory really have terrible allergies?

Jane gave her nose a vigorous rubbing until it looked red and roughed up, and then made her way to the nurse's office.

The nurse was a sweet, round, local woman in a clean white uniform. "*Buenas tardes,*" she greeted Jane kindly. "What can I do for you?" Her accent was beautiful, like a woman used to speaking English, but in no hurry to lose her own voice.

"I'm out of my antihistamines. I guess I didn't pack enough." Jane clasped her hands and hoped to look embarrassed. "I think my friend Tory came here the other night and you helped her."

The nurse frowned. "No, no girls have come in the night."

"Oh, I must have been mistaken." Jane sat on the edge of the exam chair.

"But how could you be mistaken about something like that?" The nurse flipped through the pages of a spiral bound desk calendar. "Did she say she came here in the night?"

"I thought she did."

"Then she lied. There isn't any other place she could have gone. I lock up at eight, and nobody called me." She frowned at her calendar. "And I have the only key to my clinic."

"She's not really the kind of girl who would lie. Maybe she meant she went to see someone else. Someone who had some medicine. Maybe Ginger," Jane said.

"No. She couldn't have done that. Ginger wouldn't give out medicine. We have to be very careful here so the government doesn't catch us breaking rules. It is a difficult balance to always be pleasing the government but taking care of the children with donations. We don't always have enough, but we can't possibly break the rules."

"Would they shut you down?"

"We could not afford the official and unofficial fines they would impose on us. We must always be above board . . . No, your friend lied." She looked up at Jane and made unflinching eye contact. "I don't like liars."

Jane rubbed her nose instinctively. "She must have meant she got some from our leader, Owen. I'm sorry I bothered you. I'll go ask him."

The nurse relaxed back into her chair. "She went to the men's dorm at night? She is a bold girl, if she's not a liar." The nurse pursed her lips. "Go ask her again what she said, but if she says she came to me, don't trust her. In this world, you must be very careful who you are friends with." A light knock on the door interrupted her.

"*Bienvenidos,*" She welcomed the newcomer, a preteen boy with a scrape on his forehead. "Been climbing in the orchard again?" she asked him in Spanish.

He grinned ruefully.

"*Gracias.*" Jane thanked the nurse quietly and left.

The nurse confirmed her suspicions about Tory. She hadn't spent an evening there, and probably didn't have severe allergies. She was sneaking around, day and night, to do something she wasn't willing to admit.

But the nurse had revealed something else in her surprisingly intense talk. She was paranoid, and doing her best to teach people to be wary.

Probably a result of the abuse she was seeing and treating. If she had been reporting it to Dr. Rodriguez, she had to trust him to take care of it. And it sounded like she couldn't dare report it to the police for fear that she would bring down a punishment to the orphanage that they literally couldn't afford.

Jane considered going to Dr. Rodriguez's nice receptionist to talk about what might be in walking distance from the orphanage, and if anyone might have noticed someone leaving at night, but then she remembered the back parking lot. Perhaps Tory had gone back there that first day to case the joint, and had used that exit to slip away when she ought to have been working or sleeping.

The courtyard was quiet, the police presence was felt, but again, she wasn't stopped as she crossed the campus.

The little parking lot was empty, but the gate was locked. The cyclone fencing had razor wire running across the top. This was not a fence Tory could climb out of.

Jane jingled the gate. It was padlocked. She picked the lock up and examined it. The keyhole was very scratched up. There seemed to be, in addition to normal wear and tear, some fresh, deep scratches. A key wouldn't have made them in a normal kind of unlocking situation, but maybe it could have happened if someone had picked it.

Jane walked up and down the length of the fence. One farm house surrounded by fields, and nothing else as far as she could see. But the two lane road had to meet up with the main road somewhere along the line. At the very least, you could turn a corner somewhere and get into the village. What there was to do in the village was anyone's guess. She abandoned her search for clues and looked for Jake instead, but couldn't find him. She dearly wanted to talk out her new facts and questions, but would have to go it alone. She took herself to the dimly lit chapel, again the one room the *policia* were allowing them in that was consistently empty, and paced in the quiet, thinking and praying.

The door swung open, letting in a streak of bright sunshine and a panting Riley.

"Jane! Jane!" She rushed at Jane, grabbed her by the arm, and dragged her to a windowless corner. "Jane!"

"Riley."

"Jane, Jane, Jane!" Riley shook from head to toe. Her eyes were bulging and her face was red. "Jane!"

"I'm right here. Take a deep breath and count to three before you say my name again."

Riley inhaled, but seemed to have a problem exhaling.

"Don't hyperventilate on me. Put your hand up like this." Jane cupped her hands in front of her own nose and mouth and breathed into them.

Riley copied her. Slowly her breathing normalized. "Jane . . ."

"If you say my name one more time I'm leaving."

"J—You've got to hear what I just heard."

"That's better. What did you just hear?"

"I went to take a shower, but there were too many people in the girls' shower, so I went to the men's. No one else was in there so it really didn't make a difference. Everyone's in their designated areas, but I didn't shower yesterday so I was all sweaty and gross and stunk and it seemed like a good time to do it. Plus, the guys on the teams wouldn't like shower in the middle of the afternoon, if at all, you know? They are kind of gross, guys this age."

"Except for the showers being off limits for repairs, it does seem like showering is always a good idea."

"Oh no! Were they? I hadn't even thought of that. Oh shoot. I'm really lucky I didn't get caught. Luckier than I thought, and I had thought I was pretty lucky anyway, because when I was drying off, two men came in, but they stayed in the part by the sinks and toilets. They didn't go around the corner to the showers, so they didn't know I was there. They probably thought no one would be there because of it being off limits which makes so much sense now, but then the light was on and it was kind of steamy, so I don't know why they thought they were alone. Oh! Wait! Do you think they knew I was there and they said it to send me on the wrong track? What if it was a trap?"

Jane gauged the level of panic on Riley's face. "Don't say my name again."

"No, I won't but, Jane, Jane, Jane, what if it was a trap?"

Jane decided to ignore the name-saying. "I don't know what was said or who said it, so I can't even guess if it was a trap or not."

"It was Miguel, and some other guy who I didn't recognize. They were talking quietly, but I was paying close attention because I wanted to know exactly when they left, so I could sneak out. And Miguel was telling the other guy that they had to get Claude in the ground, as soon as possible, no matter what the people said. He said it was the most important thing right then and that they would have to push forward with it."

"But they already had the big funeral." Jane frowned. Riley was making as little sense as anyone had ever made.

"Right, but they didn't bury him. I don't know why you don't remember that. They said so in the funeral, that they were having the funeral but they didn't have permission to bury him yet because they were waiting on the people in America, his family, I think. They want to bury him because it's expensive to keep him on ice at the funeral home, but the family can't decide if they want him shipped back home or not. I heard that part over breakfast two days ago. You've really got to start paying attention, Jane. Some of this could be important!"

Jane didn't like the implication that she was bad at her job. You could only listen in to so many conversations at once, and morning wasn't her best time. Plus, they had used their funeral time wisely, she thought. So she had missed the detail about the body not being buried. Hardly a crime. "But you were saying something about a trap. Could that be a trap?"

Riley paused and narrowed her eyes. "I don't know."

"I think I'm missing something. What else did they say?"

"The other guy said he didn't see what it would help. He said it would make the police ask questions they didn't need to ask. He said that they had to remain calm, and not take any chances."

"That still doesn't sound like a trap."

Riley nodded. She pressed her hands to her knees. "Okay, yeah. Maybe not. That's good." She kept nodding, calming herself down. "Then Miguel said that they needed to meet later, at ten p.m."

"Ahh. Did he say where or what the purpose of the meeting would be?"

"They said at the far edge of the orchard, but he didn't say why." Riley stared at Jane. "That's why I was thinking it might be a trap! I knew there was a reason! I think they might have realized I was in there and wanted to lure me away."

Jane considered it. "To what end? You're a volunteer on a two-week stay. I'm sure they aren't plotting to harm you. Say Miguel is our murderer . . . you haven't given him any reason to think you suspect him, have you?"

"No! Oh no. I was just thinking if they had noticed me sneaking around, or listening in or something."

"So you maybe have given them reason to suspect you?"

"Yeah, Maybe? I don't know!" She chewed on her lip. "It's pretty exciting, isn't it?"

Jane shook her head slowly. "No. It's murder. It's dangerous and terrifying, but not exciting. Go to the lounge and hang out with the rest of the volunteers, please. I need to do some time alone.

"If I see Jake, I'll tell him what I heard." Riley hopped to her feet.

"Don't, not until I give you the heads up." Jane did not want Riley talking about what she had heard where someone might hear her. And considering her previous caution with finding the perfect place to give news, Riley's nerves were shot. A few days ago she wouldn't have told a story like that where people might have been able to listen in at the open windows.

Jane also didn't like the idea that personable Miguel was somehow involved in the death of Claude Marshall—who Jane still hoped hadn't been a murder victim.

After a considerable time in the quiet, praying, Jane sought and found her husband.

Jake was in the volunteer lounge chatting with some young men who had travelled with them. She gave him a quick nod, and he excused himself to the hall. "I can't give you details right now," Jane kept her voice low. "But you need to meet me at the gate to the orchard at exactly ten."

"Can do. Until then, you need to join me and these guys. I think you'll want to hear what we've been talking about."

Jane joined them at the threadbare overstuffed couches, and nestled into the crook of Jake's arm like it was any old day.

"Aiden here was just telling me about the trip they took here last year." Jake nodded at a kid with a hint of red in his hair. "I think the church is planning on making this an annual thing."

"Cool!" Jane smiled at Aiden. "I guess this trip is pretty different from the last one, yeah?" She shivered dramatically for effect.

"Right. Because Pat died, but also with Claude and Vanessa gone it seems weird."

"Who's Vanessa?" Jane squeezed Jake's knee. He was right to invite her to the conversation. This could be good.

"She was head of housekeeping when we were here last. I think she was engaged to Claude. I've asked about her but nobody had any real answers. Like, they changed the subject when I brought it up. Kinda weird."

"I remember Vanessa," a girl who was sitting kind of close to Aiden, but in a shy and excited way, said. "She led one of the devotions and talked about how she had ended up here and how she had been here for the last six years and how awesome it was."

"Do you remember her story?" Jane asked to draw the girl out.

"Her parents had taken them here as kids and stuff, and they had adopted a kid, too. It was all really sweet."

Jane glanced at Jake. He nodded slightly.

"What was her name again?"

"Vanessa Thompson. I remember because our fearless leader on that trip was John Thompson, He couldn't come this time."

Jane tried to keep her face a picture of calm, but was disappointed. She had been hoping the woman's name was Vanessa McBane. "Any relation to John?"

"Nope, just a coincidence. But her testimony was so, so sad. She was a super young war widow, and stuff. She talked about how being the bride of Christ had comforted her when she was super sad, and how being at the orphanage gave her children to love, and she hinted at a new romance, but didn't come out and say who it was with."

"But everyone could tell." As if the romantic story had put Aiden in the mood for his own love story, he scooted a little closer to the shy girl. "Just the way they looked at each other was enough."

The girl nodded. "So, so sweet."

"It was just different last year. Everyone was happy. Having fun. None of this weirdness about dads beating kids, or people getting murdered," Aiden said with a frown.

"I think it's a spiritual attack," The shy girl said.

"Probably so," Jake agreed.

Jane squeezed his knee again. "I've got to run, see you at dinner?"

"Yup." He kissed her cheek, and she slipped away. Time to find Ginger and ask about Vanessa Thompson, the missing widow who Jane seriously hoped was Chase McBane's big sister.

She found Ginger in the kitchen helping with supper set up.

"Do you have a minute?" Jane leaned over the kitchen pass-through and gave Ginger a smile.

"Sure." Ginger wiped her hands on her canvas apron. "Come around here."

Jane came through the kitchen to a small office.

"What do you need?"

"I was wondering if you could tell me a little bit about some of the staff that isn't here anymore."

Ginger exhaled. "It depends. I might not know anything."

"How about some of the ladies who have been on housekeeping staff in the past." She was easing into it, knowing that Ginger was strongly on the side of Pat Bromfield's crazy parenting book.

"Like Vanessa and Jennifer?"

"We can start there." Jane smiled, trying not to let on that Ginger had hit the nail on the head on her first try.

"Jennifer was here when I got here, but only stayed a few months longer. She had to go back to Minnesota, I think there was an illness in the family." Ginger ran her hand through her hair.

The back door to the kitchen swung open. Miguel entered, flustered. "*Todo el mundo a la iglesia, por favor*. Everyone to the chapel." He exited as abruptly as he had entered.

Ginger stripped off her apron.

"What about Vanessa?" Jane leaned on the door frame of the office, not willing to leave without answers.

"Didn't you hear Miguel? We are all supposed to go to the chapel. I think it's the police thing."

"Oh, sure, but I bet we have a minute or two."

"You want to mess around with Mexican police? I don't. Come on."

She elbowed her way past Jane and hustled out of the kitchen with the other women.

Ginger had known all about some women named Jennifer who Jane didn't care about in the least. Surely she knew all about Vanessa Thompson, too. If only she could get her to talk.

CHAPTER 11

It looked like the whole orphanage from temporary volunteers to the infants were in the chapel. Two police were stationed each of the three doors, and five police, all armed, stood on the stage.

Dr. Rodriguez stood at the pulpit.

When the officers shut the doors, he spoke. "Thank you all for coming in so quickly. The police have an announcement and I will translate." He spoke first in Spanish, then English.

A scrappy little officer with a big gun stood beside Dr. Rodriguez. He spoke, and Dr. Rodriguez translated line by line. "The investigation into the death of Mr. Patrick Bromfield is over. We have concluded that he was intentionally killed by an unknown person. He will be kept at the morgue until the results from the laboratory are back. No one may leave the orphanage or Mexico, until we release you. For our visitors we will attempt to give you freedom to leave before your scheduled flights. You are now free to use all of the orphanage facilities and to resume work as usual."

The scrappy little policeman stepped back.

Dr. Rodriguez cleared his throat. "*Gracias.*" He stepped back from the pulpit, but everyone stayed glued to their seats.

No one could leave. But everyone could probably leave eventually. But right now it was a no go. But work was starting back up.

It opened up a whole world of investigation that had to begin tonight at ten, in the orchard, and really had to be wrapped up by the date on her plane ticket.

The police cleared the chapel out in an orderly manner and then stationed themselves back around the property, watching, listening, whatever. There were more of them this time, and they seemed intense.

Jane hunted for Ginger but didn't have any luck until supper, when she spotted her in the kitchen helping serve up the *pozole.*

For about ten minutes the hearty, savory soup distracted Jane from what she really needed to do, but it was worth it. *Pozole* was not something she had grown up with in her hamburger-centric family in Portland.

Jane watched Tory slip away with Chase and considered following them, but she needed Ginger's confirmation of her suspicions first. Unfortunately, Ginger hadn't stayed for supper clean up, and couldn't be found.

Jane gave up and went back to the dorm. Riley was stationed on a top bunk, her eye on Tory.

Tory was settled into her own bunk, reading a thick paperback.

The clock moved slowly. There was no lights out curfew for the volunteers since this wasn't a children's camp, but by ten they had dimmed the lights out of consideration for those who wanted to sleep. When the lights went down Jane grabbed her toothbrush and slipped away. She shoved the toothbrush in her pocket with a shrug. No one would have cared if she had walked out, but she had felt the need for an excuse.

Jake was waiting at the gate to the orchard as promised.

"Someone is meeting Miguel out here. We don't know why, or what for, but we do know it has something to do with the death of Claude. We want to be very quiet, and slip around to the far end and see what we can hear," Jane said.

Jake nodded, and led the way in silence. Jane felt like her feet were thundering over the solid turf.

The smell of smoke hit them first, and as they followed it, a small glow in the distance made it easy to find the two men. Jane and Jake hunkered behind two trees and strained to listen to the hushed voices.

"The ashes will blend in with the dirt. No one will notice anything out this far." That was Miguel. The conversation was in Spanish, but Jane was able to follow it with ease, as there were no other voices to distract her.

The other man, whose silhouette looked like Dr. Ben Rodriguez, just nodded.

"Though I can't understand why we let it go on this long."

"It was always an excuse with him," Rodriguez said. "Tomorrow, tomorrow, tomorrow, but he never did do it."

"It's over now." Miguel stomped the little blaze out and kicked the ashes around. Rodriguez did the same, kicking dusty dirt over the place the fire had been. "No record he was ever here."

Dr. Rodriguez exhaled loudly. "This is not how a Christian home should run."

Jake stepped out from behind the trees. "Well, hey there." His hands were stuffed in his pockets, and he ambled casually toward the men. "Did I miss the bonfire?" He spoke in English. They had no reason to think he had understood their conversation, but Jane knew better. While not fluent, he had the vocabulary to have gotten the gist of things.

"What can we do for you?" Dr. Rodriguez stepped away from Miguel.

"Oh, I was just wandering, enjoying our bit of freedom. Thinking about the losses you all have suffered. And wondering what exactly you were hiding."

Miguel laughed unnaturally loud. "Hiding? Come on. Let's get back in."

"How long have you been out there?" Dr. Rodriguez did not follow Miguel's call to leave.

"Long enough. Was that Claude's file you burned up just now?"

Jane kept her place behind the tree. The way Dr. Rodriguez seized up when Jake asked his question made her think she would be more valuable as a surprise, if needed.

"My wife and I are here on official business." Jake pulled out his wallet, though Jane didn't have a clue what he was showing them. "We're private detectives who have been hired by Victor Trives—you may have heard of him—to follow his daughter and Chase McBane, the rock star. I think you'd better tell me what's going on."

Dr. Rodriguez's shoulders relaxed. "It has nothing to do with those two, I promise."

"Help me see why."

"Claude, you see, he just kept forgetting to get his papers in order. He had been here illegally for almost five years."

"But he's dead now, so what could that matter?"

Dr. Rodriguez stepped closer. "I don't know. It could be fine, but it might not be. If we have no record of him at all, there isn't any expired visa for the police to find, is there?"

"You're right," Jake said. "That's not how a Christian home should operate."

"We should have let him go years ago, but he was very talented, and dedicated."

"He was a great guy, but terrible with paperwork."

"It sounds like it."

Dr. Rodriguez laughed softly. "You can see how we are just doing this because of the investigation, right? It has nothing to do with your job."

"I can see why you are doing it, but it's up to Jane to decide if it has anything to do with her case. I'm just her heavy," He said it lightly, and the two men laughed. "Why don't we three join Jane in your office, Doctor, and we can talk about it more."

Dr. Rodriguez stiffened again, perhaps not enjoying the pretentions Jake had taken. "I think we've spoken about this enough."

Jake shrugged. "If that's what you want." He tipped an invisible hat at the men and disappeared into the darkness in the opposite direction he had come from. Jane lost sight of him, but kept her eye on Dr. Rodriguez and Miguel.

"Why did you tell him everything?" Miguel asked. He spoke in Spanish again.

"Because I knew something was unusual with McBane and that girl, and I didn't like the looks of Jane and Jake either."

"But now they will put it in their report."

"I'm not concerned with a private investigator from Oregon. I'm concerned about the police, here. Those two won't report to the police, and now they know there's nothing to report. Like Jake said, Claude is gone. His immigration status doesn't matter."

The two men walked silently back toward the orphanage buildings.

They hadn't shown any sign that they noticed Jane, so the conversation they had had in private seemed to support their confession to Jake.

She kicked at the ashes herself for a while after they were gone, but the papers had been thoroughly destroyed. Nothing left to say who Claude was, where he had come from, or why he hadn't been in a hurry to sort out his paperwork.

The next morning Jane smelled like the smoky remains of a camp fire. She thought about wearing it as a badge that she was onto Miguel, but couldn't take the stink for very many minutes after she woke up. She hit the showers—the correct showers—and joined her team for breakfast, fresh as a daisy. They only had a few days left to untangle the mess. If they had chore assignments for the day, she wasn't sure that she could get the job done.

Breakfast was eggs, beans, hot sauce, tortillas, oranges and little cinnamon rolls. She appreciated the treat and helped herself to three of them with her coffee.

Jake was nowhere to be seen so she slipped a fourth into the pocket of her hoody. The kids at her table were rambunctious, excited by the freedom, by the weight that had been lifted with the police announcement the day before. Conversation buzzed with what they hoped to get done today, everything from sharing the gospel with the little kids, to making progress on the building project. The excitement was contagious, so when Miguel announced that the orphanage had decided to have voluntary limited freedom she was also disappointed. Dorms, lounge, chapel, cafeteria, and the building project were open. The team leaders would help their own volunteers figure out where they could best help. The school-age kids were staying home again, as everyone was required to remain on the property, and Miguel hoped that the groups would offer some worship and Bible study in the chapel.

Jane hadn't had much to do with their leader Owen, but she hoped he'd respect her position and not sign her up for anything in particular.

Her hope was in vain, so she nabbed Owen after his brief meeting.

"Owen, you remember why Jake and I are here, right? Trives and Flora Wilson arranged for us to come on this trip with a specific purpose in mind."

Owen smiled at Jane, in a way she could only consider condescending. "They may have had one purpose, but God has one, too."

"I need access to Tory and Chase if I am going to fulfill my obligation to my boss. You need to quit putting us on the opposite side of the orphanage from each other."

"Calm down. You'll see each other again at lunch."

"I recognize as youth pastor of Faith Freedom Church you have a responsibility on this trip, but when you agreed to have a private investigator join the team, you accepted that responsibility as well."

He leaned back in his chair, getting comfortable. "I was assured by your boss that you were a devout young woman who would be not only willing, but excited to serve with the team."

What really stung about his attitude was that Jane knew she was at least two years older than Owen.

"Trust and obey, Jane. Be faithful in the little things and you will be entrusted with greater things." He smiled benignly, and didn't move, waiting for her response.

Jane also remained silent. The tone he had taken grated at her in a deep place. His superiority, his belief that her cleaning the dorms would be such a great service to the orphanage that it outweighed her investigation, his staring at her and not saying anything at all.

He sat back, one leg crossed over the other, his arms resting on the arms of the chair. He was the picture of confidence. She considered his posture and his position at length. A church leader, but probably only part time. Young, in charge of the group. He wasn't the head of the team last time, just another teammate, like the rest of the kids. There was just that air of unearned authority about him that fit in so well with the troubles at the orphanage. "So," she said after a lengthy stretch. "You said you come here a lot, right?" She settled into her chair, mimicking his body posture.

"This is my second trip this year. Seventh total." He looked pleased with himself.

"You really love it here, don't you?"

"Absolutely."

"Losing Pat, Claude and Vanessa, must have been hard."

He froze, a look of confusion on his face. "I really didn't know them well."

"Oh no? I had the idea that folks from Faith Freedom were well acquainted with Claude Marshall and Vanessa Thompson."

He shook his head, but a red blush was beginning to crawl up his cheeks. "I don't think so."

"No? Aiden sure remembered them well. And Aiden's girlfriend. Of course, I suspect Chase McBane knows Vanessa even better than you do."

Owen's jaw clenched, but his face was mostly a picture of confusion. "I don't know what you're getting at. I didn't know any of them. I just come here for the kids." He gripped the arms of his chair as though to stand, but hesitated.

"I'm sure we all do." Jane chuckled. "Except for Jake and I, of course. But before you go, what have you heard of Vanessa Thompson? She seems to have disappeared into thin air, just like Claude Marshall."

"I don't know anything. I swear. I come to serve the kids and to help the youth from our church grow. This trip has been a real mess, but I didn't do anything." He looked sick to his stomach, and when he stood, he wavered on his feet. "You have an assignment, just like the rest of us. If you don't want to do it, I can't make you, but that's on your conscience." He walked out slowly, as though he had to pull himself together.

Perhaps Jane's questions had hit too close to home, but if so, she was surprised. She had expected him to sing the praises of Pat and his parenting books, and his life philosophies, not collapse at the mention of the two dead men and one missing woman.

The trouble now was to find someone who knew anything about this Owen character who would be willing to spill the beans.

CHAPTER 12

Jane spotted Miguel in the far corner of the cafeteria. The room was clear but for two girls wiping down the tables. She took a seat across from him and smiled gently. "Are you hanging in there?"

He shook his head. "I haven't had one minute to grieve over *mi amigo* Pat."

"You two were close?"

"Yes. He was a great mentor. He taught me so much about how to be open and honest, and to feel things strongly."

Jane wondered how hard that might have been, since Miguel seemed like that kind of Christian guy who wears his heart on his sleeve.

"And now I can't even sit and cry over the man who told me it was okay to cry."

"That's rotten. But cool that he was a sensitive guy." Cool, and completely at odds with the other things she had heard.

"He taught me that emotions were a strength, if you harnessed them, and didn't let them harness you. Cry when you hurt, and get up and do a good work. That was his mission, his message.

But has anyone had a chance to cry for him? No. We've been too busy trying not to get arrested."

"Do you know what makes them think it was murder?" She wondered if anyone else had been given the clues Jake had been given, and if so, what they made of them.

He looked side to side, then locked eyes with Jane. "I know you're a private detective."

"That's okay. I don't mind. I was just wondering why they had concluded murder."

"I think it is something they learned from the mmm, *autopsia.* I'm sorry. I don't know that word in English. *"*

"It's the same. Autopsy. But what did they find, I wonder."

"They didn't tell us. But you saw the body, what did you think?" Miguel had his eyes locked on Jane, as though he hoped she could ease his mind of his fears.

"I thought he died a completely nonviolent death, if that is any comfort. Whether it was a stroke, or poison, or whatever, he went, well, kind of peacefully, I guess."

"I hope so. For him."

"You guys say goodbye a lot around here don't you?" It was time to maneuver the conversation towards Vanessa.

"People don't usually die here."

"But there is a lot of coming and going. Short term groups, volunteers, that kind of thing."

"Yes. You are right. There is a lot of coming and going. Sometimes it's harder than others."

"I bet Pat was good at helping you guys handle that, dealing with the grief and stuff."

"That's exactly what started it. He could see we were hurting, and helped us learn to feel the pain, to grieve, but to keep working. We have some groups that come year after year, you know? We're close with these people. When they leave, it is terrible. But Pat helped."

"And when folks come for a few years and then just disappear?"

"That can be even harder. Depends on the person." He seemed to relax a little, as though he had heard what he wanted to hear. That Pat hadn't suffered.

"I hear it was hard for Claude when Vanessa Thompson left."

"That was terrible. She disappeared. One day she was gone. And he was left with a broken heart. Claude was not a man to give his heart easily."

"What was Claude like?"

"He was the opposite of Pat. Tough on the outside, but soft on the inside. A man of few words. He fell deeply in love with Vanessa, but moved slowly. He'd never been married, you see, and she was widowed. He didn't want to hurt her, but also didn't seem to know how to romance her. Like a young boy, almost."

"That's so sweet."

"Except the night she vanished. That wasn't so sweet. Not even a goodbye to him. Or anyone. He didn't speak for days."

"Did Pat help him with his grief?" Jane wanted to reach a hand across the table to comfort Miguel, she was so grateful for his open conversation.

Miguel shook his head, but smiled. "No, they were like oil and water. Claude took two weeks off, did a little travelling, and then came home, much better off."

"He got over her in two weeks?"

"I wouldn't say that, but he was more his old self."

"Gosh. This place is a regular soap opera."

"*Telenovela.* This is Mexico, after all."

"Was all of that years ago?"

"No. It was this summer. Claude had only been home a month when he died."

Facts spun through Jane's mind like cards in an old fashioned rolodex. Bits of information flashing past her mind's eye, finding their spot in the big picture.

Vanessa with the adopted sister.

Chase with the adopted sister.

Claude who was dead who had loved Vanessa.

Pat who was dead who had been Claude's opposite, maybe even enemy, who also seemed to be a really bad father.

The women telling their stories safely, in knotted string.

The teenagers angry at Pat for how their sisters were treated.

Sisters, adopted, orphaned, and missing.

Mothers, plotting, hoping, scheming.

And those knotted strings—they just had to be the key to how and why.

"What did Vanessa's family say about her disappearance?" Jane asked.

"It was very strange. they didn't say anything. She didn't have any kids, of course, but we had contact information for her parents. Dr. Rodriguez called them and talked, but, I don't know. I would have expected them to be very upset. To contact police, and newspapers, television maybe, but I never heard a word."

Jane doubted the phone call had been made. Vanessa, like her true love Claude, seemed to be another person who had never existed at the orphanage. Her file was probably ashes in the orchard, maybe her body, as well.

After a sullen dinner, Jane and Jake found themselves pacing up and down the aisle in the chapel. "I don't see how we can take that next step without involving the police." The words stuck in Jane's throat, but as soon as she heard herself say them she had a different perspective. "But if I worked it right, it would be like the police were my tools."

"I sort of love this perspective." Jake stopped and perched on the arm of a pew. "I love your independent streak. It's very sexy in a wife. But I hate to see you fight against a system that is built to help solve crimes."

"I haven't really been fighting against the police."

"No, but you have maintained a healthy, respectful distance, and in this case, I think you need to make friends."

"I agree. I need to tell them what I have heard here, so they can help me out with what they know. We need to discuss the missing Vanessa Thompson with them, at the very least."

"Don't get your hopes up about them telling you anything, but yeah. If no one else is talking about this missing woman, you should tell them."

"Do you remember what Claude Marshall died of?" Jane switched the subject abruptly.

"Didn't he have some pre-existing thing?"

"He died of a heart condition. I'm sure that's what Miguel said."

"We should find someone and confirm it." Jake stood up again, his feet slightly apart, arms flexing a little.

"It's a big coincidence, yes? Claude dying of a heart condition, and Pat dying because of his heart medicine . . ." Jane turned around at the altar and faced Jake.

"Are you thinking that we have a murderer with just one trick up his sleeve?"

"It sounds like it, but why? If Claude and Pat were opposites, and didn't really like each other even, why would someone kill both of them?"

"Maybe they knew something about what had happened to Vanessa. You don't have to be on the same side to have the same dangerous knowledge." Jake joined his wife, and put his hand gently on her back.

"You're right. Let's find ourselves a policeman and an interpreter. We have a potential serial killer here." Jane went straight to the door and walked into the setting sun of the late afternoon.

Jake followed, close at hand.

A young officer stood at attention on the corner of the courtyard nearest the chapel. He had his eyes on nothing in particular, as far as Jane could tell, but was probably trying to watch all of the doors at once.

Jane paused, squared her shoulders, and marched to the officer. "*Hola, señor. Por favor, yo tengo…. *"

The office stared at her, looking bored.

She hesitated too long and couldn't pull the words out she needed, though they were common enough. She reverted to English with an apologetic shrug. "I need to tell you something. About the murder. I think it might be important."

He narrowed his eyes and tilted his head. "Yeah? What is it?" He didn't even have an accent.

She sighed. "Oh! Good. You speak English. This is Jake, the cops think he might have done it, and I'm his wife, and we have something we need to tell you."

Jake took a step back, his hands up. "Wait a second."

She turned her face slightly and mouthed the words "Trust me."

The officer pulled out a walkie-talkie and let off a string of fast Spanish police jargon.

Someone responded.

Jane's heart beat like a hammer against her ribs.

"Okay, come on then." The officer looked like he wanted to take them away to talk about as badly as he wanted to go to the dentist, but he led them up to the director's office anyway.

"The *comandante* said I could take your statement, since my English is the best of us here. He doesn't want to talk to you again, unless he has to."

"The feeling is mutual." Jake took the seat that Dr. Rodriguez silently offered him.

Jane took the chair next to her husband, but sat on the edge of it.

Dr. Rodriguez was ushered out of his office, and the officer shut the door behind him.

"What's your problem? You talked your way off the suspect list. Did you want back on it?"

"Of course not. But I think you might have three murders to solve, not just one." Jane bit her lip.

The officer sighed. "Do you watch a lot of police shows back home?"

Jane ignored the insult. "First, a woman named Vanessa Thompson disappeared without a trace. Then a man named Claude Marshall died of complications from a heart condition. And finally Pat Bromfield also died of complications from a heart condition. Possibly caused by someone messing with his medicine. I think Claude's death was also caused by someone messing with his medicine."

The officer didn't roll his eyes, but it was close. "And what evidence do you have of this?"

"None."

"No evidence that the woman is dead? No evidence that the other man's medicine was tampered with?"

"With two men dead in such short space of time, dying of the same thing, surely you were already considering the possibility they were connected, right?"

"I'm here to make sure no one leaves the orphanage. Not to consider possibilities. That's for the *comandante.*"

"He said you were supposed to take my statement, right? I want to make an official statement so you guys will look into it." Jane nodded her head as she spoke trying to get him to agree with her.

"You just did. You stated it. Now go back to whatever you were doing so I can go back to what I was doing." He looked at the clock, but didn't open the door.

"I suspect you are hoping we might make it worth your while to tell the *comandante* what we just told you." Jake spoke slowly and pulled out his wallet.

"Are you trying to bribe me?" The officer laughed.

Jake held his wallet but kept it closed. "It depends. Are you asking for a bribe?"

"No. I'm asking you to quit bothering me." He let himself out.

Dr. Rodriguez entered his office. "What do you want to know about Vanessa?" He took his chair behind his desk, and folded his hands in front of him.

"Everything. Is she Chase McBane's sister?" Jane cut straight to point.

"I don't know. You would have to ask him."

"Why did she leave?"

"I don't know. You would have to ask her."

"Where did she go?"

"The answer is the same. She didn't tell anyone that she was planning to leave, much less where to or why."

"What did her family say when you called them?"

He frowned. "They were remarkably calm. They said thank you for the information. I got the impression that they knew about it beforehand."

"Did you really call them?" Jake was lounging in his chair, as though he had no cares in the world. "Because that story sounds a bit like a lie."

Dr. Rodriguez's face turned red. "Of course it does. The truth often sounds false, but it's true. You can call them yourselves if you want to."

"Okay." Jane smiled.

Dr. Rodriguez cleared his throat.

"Let me guess," Jane said. "Her file is fertilizing the orchard."

"We may have retired her information permanently." He struggled to say it.

"This is not how you want to run a Christian orphanage, is it?" Jane asked softly.

He shook his head. "No. Things have gotten out of hand."

"Since Pat introduced his parenting book?" Jane continued with the soft, understanding voice.

"I couldn't say. All I know is that we need to regroup. To pray and seek guidance. Because no, making files disappear is not a good thing. But if you knew what we had to deal with to keep volunteers coming with ease, to be allowed to take children in, to be able to feed them. We can't get on the wrong side of the police, and sometimes that involves doing things that don't feel right."

"But are for the greater good. Like the midwives in Exodus," Jake said.

Dr. Rodriguez gave Jake a thankful look. "Exactly like that."

Jane stood up. "Thank you. I guess now we go talk to Chase and Tory."

"This investigation will be over soon. You'll fly home and forget about it, and that will be for the best." Dr. Rodriguez stood up and nodded at them, indicating they should indeed go talk to someone else.

Just outside the door to the office, Jane pulled out her cell phone. Flora answered on the first ring. "*Buenos días!* I need some help."

"Rocky can be there immediately. Two days, tops."

"It's not come to that yet, but we have a missing American woman situation to go with our two murders. I was hoping you could find some contact information for her family."

"Two murders? What did I miss?" Flora's tone sounded more like "what am I missing out on?"

Jane worried that she'd never get a good assignment like this again if she made it sound too exciting. "Oh, nothing much, but it sure would help if we could get in touch with Chase's parents. They live in St. Louis, I think. They ought to also be the parents of Vanessa Thompson, née McBane."

Flora was silent, but Jane heard typing. "McBane's not his real last name," she finally said. "The band's website says that much, but doesn't tell us what his real name is."

"Okay, how about this: Vanessa Thompson is a youngish woman, recently widowed, husband a military man who died in action. That ought to have made the news."

"I can work with that. You want her parents' contact information?"

"Yes, please."

"It will take a little longer since I'll be searching newspapers. But I'll text you the names and numbers as soon as I have them."

"Thank you so much. I'm sorry to interrupt your case." Jane hadn't realized before what a blessing having a team to work with could be. Between Riley and her enthusiasm and Flora and her experience, she was going to crack this case.

"Meh. It's just insurance fraud. It might be my bread and butter, but it's not all that exciting. I'll get in touch." Flora hung up, Jane thought, happy to be involved.

Jake hadn't waited politely while Jane made her call, and it took her a while to track him down again.

He had found himself a table full of volunteers in the cafeteria.

Jane poured herself a coffee from the big aluminum pot and joined them.

"We're working out a plan for a post-siesta Bible study with the kids," Jake said. "Remember, the staff is hoping we can provide some activities since they can't go to school right now."

"Of course." Jane kissed him lightly on the back of the neck. "I've got to go have a chat with Owen. I'll find you when I'm done."

Aiden looked up from a paper he was writing on. "I think I saw him in the lounge."

"Awesome, thanks."

Jane headed straight there.

CHAPTER 13

Owen wasn't pleased to see Jane.

"If you don't mind, I'd love to have a chance to chat again." She smiled softly, a natural at the calm, quiet voice and face.

He was surrounded by volunteers from both teams, constrained to be polite when he clearly wanted to tell her to leave him alone. "Okay." He stood up awkwardly.

"Let's walk." She went along beside him, leading him to the courtyard where they could pace in circles indefinitely.

"You were upset when I brought up Claude and Pat and Vanessa. Why? Please help me."

He took a long, deep breath. "Because it's none of our business."

"That's not why."

He kept walking with her, even though she had no power over him, a good enough clue to her that he knew something and that he wanted to get it off his chest.

"You did know them well, after coming here so often. Why did you say you didn't?"

"There are police everywhere, looking for a reason to arrest someone."

"But they couldn't arrest you for anything. A short term visitor? Even one who's been here a lot."

"They fingerprinted me."

"They fingerprinted all of us." Jane changed their direction slightly, so they'd be farther away from the open windows of the various building, and slowed her steps down. "Why are you afraid?"

"I have a lot of friends here and I care about them all. I want to work here someday. When I'm done with seminary. They need a full time pastor."

"Would they hire an American?"

"I'm praying they will, but so far it's been a no. Too many Americans on staff already."

"A ha."

He stopped. "But just because I want to work here and can't, that's not a reason to kill somebody. Not a reason to kill three people."

"With Claude and Pat and Vanessa all gone there are only a few gringos left on staff."

"Just Dr. Rodriguez and Ginger." Owen's voice cracked. "But the police don't know I want to work here, and they don't know I've been refused. They don't need to know it, so don't tell them."

"I don't have any reason to tell them. I can see why you didn't want anyone to think you had a connection with the three of them. But Owen, the staff here surely knows what your relationships were since you've been here so many times."

"It was a mistake to lie." His face was ashen, and he stumbled as he walked. He hadn't confessed everything yet.

"Sit down with me." Jane gestured to a bench under an awning on the windowless side of a storage building. "What else is going on."

He rubbed his jaw with a shaky hand. "I love these people. I loved Claude and Pat, and I thought Vanessa was terrific. I hate that I said I didn't know them. I love the rest of the staff here, too, and I don't want to see anyone punished for anything."

"Even murder?"

"It can't have been murder. Everyone is mistaken." He stared into the distance, his eyes locked on the men's dorm.

"What else are you wanting to say? Please tell me."

He took another deep breath, so deep Jane was afraid he might pass out.

"I hid the bag of pills in our dorm."

Jane was frozen.

"The nurse gave them to me. Told me I had to help her. Told me to just hide them anywhere, but not to flush them."

"The nurse did?" Jane spoke slowly. The nurse who hated liars?

"Yes. She said, she said . . . medicine is valuable, that she couldn't watch it be wasted. She had taken it from someone, caught someone with it. Someone trying to destroy it and she had saved it. She had promised to make it disappear."

"Why had she turned to you for help?"

"She's my friend. She knows she can trust me. She said the police had already searched our things and wouldn't do it again. She promised me they wouldn't. She said if I would take them and hide them, I could give them back right before we left. It would be easy, simple even, and I might save someone's life."

"Did you hide them in Jake's bag?" She threw out her suspicion, expecting him to correct her if she was wrong.

"I tucked them into the empty bunk above his. Between the mattress and the bed frame."

"You should tell the police." She continued in a slow, quiet almost sing-song voice, to calm him and keep him listening.

"I can't do that to the nurse. She'd be arrested."

Jane thought about that. She would be arrested, and who knew what that would mean for her or the orphanage. But if she had rescued the pills from destruction, she knew who the killer was.

Jane could take the information to the police, or ask the nurse to, but she couldn't keep it to herself. "Okay. I understand. I won't tell the police. Perhaps you could admit to hiding them. Maybe you thought they were something else."

"No. They would arrest me and I'd get kicked out of seminary. No way."

Jane was beginning to lose her patience with Owen. She had estimated him as about two years younger than herself, but he seemed less mature than Tory right now. She wanted to give him a good swift kick in the pants and make him buck up, but that wouldn't do. She just didn't have the kind of personality that could rally a person to admit to the *policía* that they had hidden evidence. "Okay.

You've told me now, and you are going to have to trust me with the information. I'm a professional with a job to do. Don't freak out and do something stupid." She stood up and walked slowly away. She was headed back to the nurse, but didn't like it one bit.

The nurse, so the receptionist at the main office said when asked, was home sick. How she had gone home when the orphanage was considered closed, Jane did not know. She was also surprised to learn the nurse lived off campus. Surprised, disappointed, and severely aggravated. But she didn't have time to worry about that for long.

Two police officers swept past her with Jake in tow. They managed to scoop her up in their wake, and shoved everyone into Dr. Rodriguez's office, whether the doctor wanted them or not.

One man was the scrappy little officer with the big gun who had made the announcements the day before. He stood over the other police officer—the one who hadn't wanted to be bothered—seething.

The officer who hadn't wanted to be bothered sat in a folding metal chair in front of Dr. Rodriguez's secondhand metal desk, with Dr. Rodriguez seated in his chair. Jane and Jake had the roomier, but threadbare, chairs against the wall. The scrappy, small officer was the *comandante*. And he was not happy. "A rich, powerful American with a motive for killing the dead man tells you he has important information, I tell you to take the statement, and you refuse to report it to me?" The commandant's voice was icy cold, and almost a hiss.

The seated officer did not reply.

"I am in charge of this investigation—the investigation into the murder of a rich American man who works for a business that brings a great deal of benefit to our town. You do not get to decide what information is worth reporting."

"Some woman went missing. Name, Vanessa. There. You have the report." The seated officer spoke in his clear English.

The *comandante* sniffed. "Hardly a report. Who is Vanessa? What did she do? How old was she? When did she leave? What was her relationship to the dead man?"

"To the two dead men," Jake volunteered.

The *comandante* slowly turned to Jake. "Two dead men?"

Jane closed her eyes. Only Jake would interrupt right now.

"You know that Pat Bromfield died under suspicious circumstances, but not so long ago, Claude Marshall died under almost exactly the same circumstances. And over the summer Marshall's fiancé went missing with no trace. She's the missing woman you are discussing."

The *comandante* turned to Dr. Rodriguez. "*Mi amigo*, what is this story?"

Dr. Rodriguez swallowed. "It is true, but . . ."

"Did you report the woman missing?"

Dr. Rodriguez kept his eyes strictly on the *comandante*. "No. Not to the *policía estatal*."

"Then you reported it to the *federales*?"

"No."

"Who, then?"

"Her family. When they weren't shocked, or concerned, we left it at that."

The *comandante* shifted his steely stare to Jake. "But you say the woman's fiancé has been killed just like Bromfield." It was a statement, not a question. "We will need to do an autopsy on this man Marshall. And I want a description of this woman. We will begin looking for her."

Jane's phone buzzed in her pocket. She wanted to check it and see if it was the contact information for Vanessa's family, but she didn't dare.

"This is all you had to say?" The *comandante* asked Jake.

"For now."

"If you know something else, you need to tell me now. Otherwise I arrest you and hold you until you decide to speak."

Jake shrugged. "That's up to you." The picture of lackadaisical insouciance

The *comandante* turned to his lazy officer. "Arrest this man, and bring him to the *delegaciones*. He'll talk if he's locked up long enough."

The officer stood up, a sickly grin on his face. "*Venga*." He grabbed Jake by the arm and jerked him up.

"You'd better just tell them whatever it is you are keeping in." Dr. Rodriguez's voice broke over his few words.

"I think I'd better not. I'd rather be the one in prison innocently if my thoughts are unfounded," Jake offered his selfless opinion as the officer dragged him out.

Jane was frozen to her chair. She didn't know where the *delegaciones* was located. Didn't know how to find a lawyer in Mexico, and didn't know if the message waiting on her phone would free her husband or not.

The *comandante* left, too. Maybe assuming that a woman wasn't worth arresting. Maybe not. But Jane decided the best option for the moment was not to draw any attention to herself. Now was not the time to rat out Owen and the nurse.

As soon as the door shut behind the *comandante*, the officer, and her husband, she pulled her phone out. She had a short message from Flora: A name—Laura Thompson—and a phone number.

Thompson?

The disappointment that rolled over Jane was palpable. Thompson was Vanessa's married name. Would her in-laws know anything at all about Chase's family?

She'd never know until she called, and this office was as good a place to call from as any.

She smiled at the grim-faced doctor and made the call.

CHAPTER 14

It took two calls and a lot of backbone to stay in her seat while Dr. Rodriguez stared at her. He didn't seem to know what to say about Jake's arrest, and as she had all of her attention focused on the phone, he didn't have much of an opening.

After what felt like an hour, but was only seven minutes of trying, someone answered the number Flora had sent.

"Is this Laura Thompson?" Jane asked as soon as she heard hello.

"Yes."

"I'm a private investigator looking into the disappearance of Vanessa Thompson. May I ask you some questions?"

"Vanessa is missing?" Laura sounded surprised.

"Unfortunately, yes." Jane caught her up with what she knew of Vanessa's story, omitting Pat's death, as it wasn't necessary for Laura. "I am trying to contact her because I think she would like to know that her fiancé has passed."

"Of course she would. She was in love with Claude."

"Laura, I don't have a relationship listed for you in my file, do you mind clearing that up, just for my notes?"

"I'm her sister-in-law. She was married to my brother."

"Thanks. When was the last time you heard from her?"

"In August. She emailed me to say that Claude had proposed. No ring or date, but you know, being a missionary, they don't have a lot of money."

"Of course. Did she say anything about going away soon?"

"Not to me. I'm sorry."

"Is it unusual to go so long between talking to her?"

"Not really. We keep in touch, but not daily or anything." Laura sounded honestly worried, which didn't match with Dr. Rodriguez's report.

"I really appreciate you talking to me. I just have another question, if you don't mind. Do you think anyone has talked to her parents or her brother?" Jane crossed her finger. If Vanessa wasn't Chase's brother, or didn't have a brother at all, that little comment could kill the conversation.

"Golly, I don't know. I haven't talked to any of them in years. But I think her parents are at the same number still. Do you have it?"

"I don't, but I sure would like it if you don't mind."

"Of course." Laura read off a phone number.

"What about her brother? Were they close? Might she have contacted him?"

"I couldn't say, I'm sorry. He was a kid when I knew him, and now he's so busy, on tour all the time and everything. I suggest you contact her parents. Vanessa's usually so thoughtful. If she's okay, she's talked to them, I just know it."

And, confirmed. Chase and Vanessa were brother and sister.

"Thank you Laura, you have been incredibly helpful. This is my number where you can contact me if you want to, and the number of my boss if you want to confirm anything I've said." She gave Laura the information and ended the call. Her phone was hot in her shaking hand. She was so close now.

It seemed obvious Chase had come to the orphanage because his sister was missing. That part was clear, job done. Tory cleared from wrongdoing, Chase cleared as a respectable boyfriend.

She'd just have to find out what had happened to Vanessa, which ought to topple the dominoes of the two murders, too.

"I called her parents and spoke to them. I've told you this already. I am a man of integrity." Dr. Rodriguez's hands clenched in white-knuckled fists.

"I really want to believe you, but I think I have few questions for them that you might not have thought to ask at the time she went missing."

Jane dialed, and prayed, and hoped that this call would be the one that solved everything.

"Hello?" The voice that answered Jane's call was thin and fragile, like a sweet grandmother. But she hadn't identified herself, and Jane, in her effort to sound like she already knew the family, hadn't asked Laura for Vanessa's mother's name.

"Good afternoon." She started simple, and honest. "My name is Jane, and I've been working with Chase recently." First mistake. McBane wasn't his real last name. Chase might not be his real first name, either. She held her breath.

"Oh, isn't that nice." There was a smile in the voice that made Jane relax.

"Am I speaking to his mother?" Jane asked.

"Oh no, dear. I'm his grandmother, Martha. Raelene isn't in right now. May I take a message?"

"Oh, that's kind, thank you. Maybe you could help me out if you had a minute." Jane cursed her luck—grateful in reality that she didn't have the power to curse things or have to rely on luck, but nonetheless severely disappointed. "I'm trying to get a hold of Vanessa. She has been active in the work we are doing, but I can't seem to track her down."

"Oh, no, you wouldn't be able to." Martha's voice was sad. "We haven't heard from her in the longest time."

"Is everything okay?"

"She said so, but Mexico is such a dangerous place. I just hate to think of her out there all alone. She should have never left the orphanage."

Jane considered her next question carefully. "Did she say when you would be able to reach her again?"

"She didn't tell me, but she might have told Raelene. I don't really know. She just said she had to go somewhere she wouldn't have phones or computers for a while, but that she would be fine. I just hate it when young people do this to us. No consideration for their worried relatives." There was a soft humor to her statement as though she knew that Vanessa was plenty old enough to take care of herself, but worried anyway.

"Well that puts us in the same position, doesn't it? Wondering and full of questions but forced to wait."

"I'm sure it does. I'm sorry I couldn't help you. You should ask at the orphanage where she used to work. She said they were sending her to help a new location, in the jungle I think, but why there would be orphans in the jungle I'll never know." She paused. "Oh dear, maybe forget I said that, would you? She said they weren't supposed to talk about it yet, but that she felt like her mother and father would want to know. I'm sorry. Don't mention it to Chase, dear. He is so protective of her. May I take your name and number and have my daughter call you back? She should be here by seven."

"Of course, thank you." Jane gave Martha her name and cell phone number. "You can let her know I'm trying to contact Vanessa if you'd like. And thank you for the conversation, I'll keep the information to myself." She ended the call and stared at her phone.

Dr. Rodriguez didn't give her any time to consider what she'd heard. "If you've just learned something regarding a missing persons case that you yourself have instigated, you obviously cannot keep it to yourself."

"Did you send Vanessa to the new location to help start it up?" Jane asked.

"Of course not. We do our very best to start every work with native Spanish speakers, for the sake of the children." He looked offended.

"I thought not." She let herself out of his office. It sounded like Vanessa left of her own will, but the why and where hung like an anchor around Jane's neck.

Out of the office in the bright sun, Jane realized that she couldn't run to her husband to go over what she had heard. He had let himself get arrested. She also couldn't go to the police station to bail him out since she had no idea where it was, no transportation to get to it, and no money to pay the bail. He'd have to sit and simmer for a while. It would probably be good for him, though the idea was very unpleasant to Jane.

Owen was an empty vessel, and too shaken to be of any real use right now. Miguel was a potential suspect in the troubles. Ginger was on the side of the weird parenting book. It looked like she'd have to try and connect with Esperanza and Riley, the two young ladies who had the right attitude toward the situation.

Riley and Esperanza were both in the lounge of the teen house, playing cards. Jane caught Riley's eye first. She gave her head a jerk, indicating she wanted to talk privately.

Riley dropped her cards and hopped up.

Jane sidled up to Esperanza. "Could I steal you from the game for a moment?"

Esperanza lifted an eyebrow. "*Bien*." She laid her cards down with care and followed Jane outside, where Riley had gone to wait.

"Ladies, I'm in a bit of trouble, and could use your help." The three of them walked across the courtyard, toward the orchard. "As Riley knows, I've been hired to find information on Chase McBane and Tory Trives, two of the volunteers here for this trip. I've learned quite a bit, but I've run into some trouble."

"*Interesante.*" Esperanza held her hands behind her back. "I was wondering why you had so many questions for us."

"Esperanza, do you remember a volunteer named Vanessa Thompson?"

"Of course I do."

Jane took a deep breath. "Chase McBane is her brother."

"Ahh." Esperanza nodded. "I had also wondered why a famous man from America had come here to spend a few weeks with no reporters or television crew to film it."

"It seems to me that he came here to find out what happened to his sister."

Esperanza was silent.

"What did Vanessa think of the book that Pat Bromfield had been teaching?"

They had reached the gate to the orchard before Esperanza spoke. "She was opposed to its use. She was very vocal with Dr. Rodriguez and the other staff. She fought against it, but the book's message was being welcomed by so many that women who wanted to fight were considered a problem."

"Even to Dr. Rodriguez?"

"It seemed so."

"So she left?"

Esperanza was silent again.

Riley had been bouncing along beside them, in pained silence, clearly wanting to talk. "I think she got smuggled out in the dark of night, don't you? Like, some others who supported her snuck her away so she could be safe, someone had threatened her, but who, and how?"

Esperanza stopped. "Who would have threatened her?" The question was asked like a teacher would do it—as though Esperanza knew the answer but wanted Riley to find it for herself.

Riley dug the toe of her shoe into the ground. "Who first brought this book to the orphanage? Was it Pat?"

Esperanza smiled. "Yes, he wrote it, even, though it is anonymous. Boxes of them come to him from America once or twice a year. He hands them out to all of the men he meets in town. He has given them to all of the parents. All of the volunteers. He is passionate about this book. This . . . idea that women must make up what is lacking in relationship to Christ's suffering, but I think he misunderstood what *San Pablo* meant when he wrote that."

"I agree," Jane said. "*God's Way for Girls and Boys* cannot be what the apostle Paul meant by his words. Vanessa, and so also Claude, were violently opposed to the philosophy that Pat had brought to the orphanage."

"Yes."

"Could Pat have killed for it?"

Esperanza shook her head. "According to his book, there is no amount of suffering a girl can do that would truly make up for bringing sin into the world, and yet, you have to keep suffering for it, so I don't think he would have killed Vanessa."

"But he might have made a really horrible threat that scared her off. Made her think that he could, um, create like, the worst suffering ever," Riley said. "Like, maybe he could have, um, I don't know. Maybe he could have threatened to break her up from Claude? Make it so they couldn't get married?"

"But would that be enough to run away?" Jane mused. If Pat had known that Claude's papers weren't in order, he could have held that over Vanessa's head, but running away from your boyfriend seemed like a worse fate than not getting to marry him. So what else might it have been?

"What if he threatened Claude? Like what if he told her that he could hurt Claude and there was nothing she could do about it and that he would do it if she didn't leave? Maybe he did that." Riley was excited like a puppy and the ideas spilled out of her.

"Yes. What if? What if he threatened to get Claude deported . . . or better, arrested?"

"*Es posible.*" Esperanza spoke softly. "Yes. If Pat had threatened Claude with arrest . . . I think Vanessa would have run away to protect him. But what could Claude have been arrested for?"

"That's easy," Jane said "He had let his visas expire. An unscrupulous cop could arrest him and hold him for ransom or whatever the worst case scenario is. He would have been lucky to just get deported back home."

"I agree," Esperanza said. "I think that must have been what Pat had threatened."

"So, where did she go?" Jane asked. "And how do we find her?"

"Let me have conversation with *mi mamá* yes? I will meet you back here this evening, after supper, and tell you what I have learned." She held out her hand for Jane, and gave her a reassuring squeeze. "If it is safe to tell the answer, now that Pat is gone, I will make sure you learn it."

"And now that Claude is gone, too," Riley said. "You can't arrest a dead man."

Esperanza didn't respond. She turned into the orchard and walked away from the orphanage, perhaps needing to plan her conversation.

CHAPTER 15

"What do you want me to do?" Riley broke into Jane's musings. "I can do anything you want. Talk to people, listen in on people, check people's houses. I'll wear gloves. I got a pair from the kitchen."

"Follow me." She had grabbed Riley in the first place to have a second brain working the problem, and she had been worth it, but Riley was ready for action. "It's been a long time since I've had my eyes on Tory and Chase. We need to find them, and we might need to split up to do it. Do you have a cell phone on you that works down here?"

"Teresa took them before we left. She's got them all in her luggage. Sorry."

"Hmmm. Okay. I guess we'd better stay within shouting distance of each other. There aren't many places they could be."

"Except if they were where we're supposed to be we'd have seen them several times today alone."

"Good point." Jane put a little speed into her step and headed for the back parking lot behind the volunteer dorms.

She heard the fight before she turned the corner. Tory, screaming her head off, something about murders.

Jane sidled along the edge of the building so as not to be noticed. She put a restraining hand out to the enthusiastic Riley.

"We've searched this crappy little village. We've searched Ensenada. She's nowhere. What did you do with her?" Tory was on her toes, almost nose to nose with Miguel.

"Control this girl." Miguel waved his arms in frustration, and smacked Tory in the face. He jumped back, hands up, a look of horror washing over him.

"Keep your hands to yourself!" Chase bolted forward and grabbed Miguel by his shirt. He lifted him up. "Or do you beat all of the girls here, huh?" His biceps bulged. The veins in his neck bulged. "Not just the children, but the women and volunteers, too?"

Miguel wriggled in Chase's grip. "Get your hands off of me. This is a murder investigation. Are you looking to get arrested?"

"Where is my sister?" Chase threw Miguel against the dorm wall.

Miguel's head cracked on the cement block and he slid to the ground with a thump.

"Chase!" Tory stepped back, hands to her face.

"Oh crap." Chase dropped to his knees and tilted Miguel's face up. "Miguel. Miguel. You okay, man?"

Miguel's eyes fluttered open and then shut again.

Jane kept her distance, praying, and not sure exactly what intervention she should or could offer.

"Step back!" Riley jumped into the scene. "I'm a nursing student." She grabbed Miguel's wrist, and held it between her thumb and forefinger.

After a moment she fanned his face and called his name. Then she lifted up an eyelid.

He twisted his head and groaned. "Chase, run and get the nurse."

Jane interjected, "No, the nurse isn't here today. Tory, go get Dr. Rodriguez. I want to talk to Chase."

Tory looked to Chase who nodded, then she bolted.

"Don't touch him," Riley said. "He surely has a concussion and maybe a cracked skull, but he is mostly alive."

He groaned again and tried to lean forward.

"Ah, ah!" Riley cautioned. "Hold still until the Dr. Rodriguez gets here. He'll probably call an ambulance and get you to the hospital for an x-ray. That was some noise your head made! But hey, Dr. Rodriguez isn't a medical doctor is he? It's a good thing I'm here!" Despite her frantic manners most of the time, she was calm, and still next to Miguel, his wrist still lightly between her fingers as though she wanted to keep track of his pulse.

"Chase—before Tory gets back—do you have any reason to believe your sister Vanessa is dead?" Jane turned her attention to Chase while she had the chance.

He grimaced but didn't deny it. "Just Claude's death. Why would they stop at one?"

"Who do you think 'they' are?"

"That's what I'm here to find out. But now that Pat is dead, I may never get to."

"Please, consider the question and don't speak fast: Did you tamper with Pat's medicine?"

Chase glared at her.

The sound of running feet thundered in the distance.

"No. I didn't. Neither did Tory. We weren't here to punish anyone. Just to bring my big sister home—even if it was just her remains."

One of the ladies Jane recognized from the kitchen came around the corner. "You got in a fight?" she asked Chase.

He bowed his head. "Yes, but I never meant to hurt him."

She sniffed. Then she gently took over for Riley and spoke to Miguel in quiet Spanish. She stood him up, one arm around his waist and led him away.

"Sorry," Tory said to Jane in an aside. "I was scared so I grabbed the first person I could find."

"They'll be going to the hospital now. She thinks he doesn't need an ambulance," Riley explained. "She's probably right, but you never know with head injuries, if his neck was hurt or anything." She shivered.

Chase began to pace, his head still bowed. "I did not mean to hurt him."

"He deserved it," Tory cried. "Did you see what he did to me?"

"It was an accident, Tory, I could tell when he did it, but I was so mad."

"An accident? He smacked me across the face." She was fuming. "And he probably killed your sister."

"Stop." Jane stepped in. "I don't believe Vanessa is dead. You are right, she's not in town and she's not in Ensenada, or probably in any of the surrounding towns. Chase, have you spoken with your mom or your grandma about Vanessa?"

He jerked his head up. "I've asked but they don't say anything."

"I talked to your grandma today, Vanessa told them she was headed to the jungle. I think I know why, but I'm not sure that we'll be able to find her." Jane turned toward the quiet orphanage glowing in the golden arms of the setting sun. "And I think I know who killed Claude and who killed Pat. Come with me." The pieces had come together. Her subconscious had been hard at work playing with the information until it was clear that there was only one answer to all of the questions. "Let's go to the sewing room."

She led the way.

Esperanza was already there with three of the housemothers, having a heated argument in Spanish.

"Sit down and keep quiet," Jane instructed Chase, Tory, and Riley. "Esperanza, I have a theory I want to run past the women. They can confirm or not, as they see fit. But Chase deserves answers, and so do Vanessa, Claude, and even Pat, because no one deserves to be murdered. Riley, will you translate?"

"*Sí.*"

"Parenting trends come and go. The one that came recently is no good, but it was catching on with the fathers and some of the younger boys, too. A whole generation of boys, in fact, was being indoctrinated."

The three mothers stared at her grimly.

"One family was actively against it, but they were sent away to a new orphanage starting much farther south. That left Vanessa, who was very vocal in her disgust, and Claude who was not vocal about anything. Also, they weren't locals, weren't married to native Spanish speakers, and weren't parents, so their voices had little impact. Or so it seemed."

She looked to Esperanza who nodded to her to continue.

"But that was just how it looked, because there were a lot of mothers who also didn't like it, but without the support of Dr. Rodriguez, there was nothing they could do. Or, very little they could do. Then Pat threatened Vanessa and Claude, so Vanessa was sent away, to the new orphanage, in the dark of night. You mothers made the plan, sharing the information with each other secretly, through an art form the men didn't know and never would. Through woman's work, so to speak." She paused and let Riley catch up. She wasn't used to being translated. "It doesn't really matter what the threat was, but I suspect it was to have Claude locked up forever. Why did Vanessa have to disappear? Why couldn't she have just gone back home like other volunteers before her? Because she wasn't done fighting the book. She had to be slipped away secretly so Pat wouldn't know where she was, so he couldn't have power over her. But she was wanted, by the mothers, because she could speak for them to the American donors, to the staff. She was sent to the same place the other dissenter was so they could work together. At least that's what I suspect happened."

One of the mothers, a small woman with dark skin and luminous eyes bit her lip, but didn't speak. The other two twisted their hands, and avoided eye contact with each other..

"Possibly Claude took two weeks to go see her and make sure she was safe. He certainly left, and came back happier, so it makes sense that he was able to confirm the love of his life was well and safe. Then he died. He didn't get arrested, as had been threatened. He died of a heart condition. It might have been murder."

"No!" The lip-biter spoke.

"It might not have been." Jane nodded. "But it gave someone the idea of how to be rid of Pat forever. Perhaps he had hurt his daughter . . . not just disciplined her, but truly harmed her with his beatings. Perhaps he had taken things one step too far."

One of the mothers in a bright red blouse, with her hair pulled back in a low ponytail nodded slightly.

"And perhaps it was his wife who did it. Not knowing when the death would occur. Just knowing that if he didn't get his treatment, maybe he too would die of his heart problem, and no one would know any better."

All three women looked away. "But he had to have some kind of pill to take, yes? And so there was a substitute in his pill bottle, and that's what the coroner found in his system."

Riley had been keeping up but looked at Jane in dismay. "I just don't know the words."

Esperanza stepped in to help.

Tears rolled down the lip-biter's cheek.

"Can you help me get in contact with Vanessa, please?" Jane switched tack. "That's all I need. About the rest, well, I am guessing it happened, but I don't know. I don't have evidence. The police have evidence. They have the autopsy. They know how to search for people who sell fake pills. They know how to interview people. I can't tell you what to do, but murder is wrong. God is the one who is supposed to bring about justice, not us." Jane was beginning to flounder. The women who sat before her were wracked with grief. Had they been in on the murder or had they tried to talk their friend out of it? Had they only guessed what Jane was thinking? She couldn't know, and they would never tell her. Their secrets were tied up in knots.

The woman in the red blouse scribbled something on a scrap of paper and passed it to Jane. A phone number.

"*Gracias, señora,*" Jane said. "I cannot tell the police my guesses, because I don't know that they are true, but I will be praying for all of you."

The looks on their faces revealed that the gist of what she was saying was the truth. And at some point, the police would get to the bottom of it, because they were trained to do that, and because these women were good, caring Christian women, they wouldn't be able to keep all of their secrets from the police, even if they would never tell Jane.

It only took an hour for the mother who had been biting her lip to follow Esperanza to Dr. Rodriguez's office. Shortly thereafter, a siren could be heard as the police arrived. Esperanza was right, secrets weren't healthy or good. And having them was no way to run a Christian orphanage.

Chase followed Jane to the chapel, but this time it wasn't empty. A whole host of children were gathered there, singing along with a band made up of the short-term volunteers. Their voices rang in the rafters, full of praise and happiness—the happiness that comes from finding a spot away from the anxious and scared adults, a spot where you can just be a kid for a while.

Jane finally settled on the volunteer lounge. She gave Chase her phone and the paper. "Call your sister. She may already know about Claude and Pat, but call her anyway. Hear her voice. Let her put your mind at ease."

"Thank you."

Despite wanting to hear everything they said to each other, Jane left to give them privacy. Besides, she still had the little problem of Jake being locked up in a Mexican prison as a person of interest in a murder investigation to sort out.

She went to Dr. Rodriguez's office again. After their little tête-à-tête she felt perfectly comfortable going to the top to request transport to get her husband out of jail.

The door was ajar, and people were talking inside. One voice in particular stood out.

Jake was lounging in a chair, his legs crossed and his arms behind his head. He laughed at something that had just been said.

A policeman, not one Jane had seen before, and Dr. Rodriguez stood across from each other with the doctor's big desk between them.

"Jane!" Jake stood up. "You really are the best. I had just gotten hold of good old Cousin Jeff to ask him to send me some big money to bribe my way out. I didn't think it would take more than five or ten thousand, but I wasn't exactly sure Jeff wanted me back that bad. How did you arrange my release from in here?" He wrapped his arms around her waist and pulled her close to kiss her cheek.

"I'd have paid twice that, Jake, but I didn't do anything to get you out."

"Sure you did. I've been sitting hear listening in to the officer and the gentleman discussing my fate for five full minutes and the only thing I could decipher was 'Jane did it' or something like that. So I know you did."

"I can only make guesses, but I think we had better slip away now and let these men sort things out."

"Hold on," Dr. Rodriguez interrupted her. "We have a situation here that you are solely responsible for." He glowered.

"I can't imagine what you are talking about," Jake said.

The police officer spoke with easy, if heavily accented, English. "I've been telling him that you are not a person of interest to us. You are free to go."

"Thanks!" Jake grabbed her hand and hoofed it outside with his wife. "But really," he said as soon as they were far from the office, "I had just dialed my lawyer to sort things out, when they dragged me back here. I did my best to follow the conversation, but it was a bit above me. The cop said I was free on new evidence. Dr.

Ben said something about you being responsible for it. I swear you must have solved the whole shebang the second I left."

"Pretty much, but I think I'll make you wait to hear how it went until I report back to Flora and Rocky."

He lifted her hand to his lips and kissed it. "How a nice kid like you could turn into a torturer, I will never know.

CHAPTER 16

Jane and Jake sat in the yellow velvet chairs across Flora's desk from her. Rocky stood to the side, leaning on the wall. "Sounds like you bit off more than you expected." His voice was growly, but his eyes were smiling."

"It wasn't the drug cartel, at any rate," Jake said.

"We work hard not to get arrested while on the job." Flora frowned at Jake. "And we never volunteer for it."

"That's not exactly true, sweetie," Rocky interposed. "Never forget Cleveland."

She turned her frown to her husband. "Cleveland is hardly Ensenada, Mexico. He had no business leaving with the police."

"You'd have to have been there," Jake said. "It really felt like the most reasonable thing at the time. Besides, Crawfords have good lawyers. Nate Goodwin. You've heard of him, I suppose."

"No."

Jane and Jake had been back for one night and a day. The last day at the orphanage had been a blur of police and crying and confusion, but that was murder for you.

Pat Bromfield's wife may have felt like her actions were justified, that she was serving a greater good, but it was still murder. And as distasteful as Pat's parenting book was, he had the right to live, to learn, and to repent from his mistakes. His wife had taken that from him, in the mistaken belief that he had killed Claude Marshall.

As far as Claude's medical records, though spotty, indicated, Pat hadn't done it. Claude had been a ticking time bomb all along.

Chase and Vanessa had had a long talk. And then Vanessa and the police had had a long talk, and then Vanessa and Dr. Rodriguez who ran the orphanage had had a long talk, the result of which was she had been sent home to St. Louis.

Bromfield's *God's Way for Girls and Boys* was banned at the orphanage now, and Vanessa was going to have to trust that God had the situation in hand.

"I spoke with Victor Trives this morning and gave him the full report," Flora said. "He is satisfied with your work. He's also a very compassionate man and the situation at the orphanage spoke to him. He has sent ten complete sets of Dr. James Dobson's parenting books, translated into Spanish, and has established a fund for a full-time chaplain, someone local who understands the culture, but who has gone to seminary so he can help everyone with their understanding of what the Bible actually says."

"That's amazing," Jane murmured. And completely unexpected. To think one man mistrusting his teenage daughter would lead to such a blessing for all of those kids and families.

"Not if you know him," Rocky said. "Old Vic's a good guy."

"Enough." Flora closed the file. "Jake, God bless you, you need to keep out of your wife's way. Understand?"

"No," Jake said with a smile.

"Relax, Flor," Rocky said. "He's a good husband. Young, but good. Don't you remember being young?"

Flora pushed her wire-rim glasses up her nose and gave her husband a very sour look.

He ruffled her grey curls. "What Flora means is that while Jane is our responsibility—that is, for the next couple of years while we are supervising her—you need to keep out of the investigations. She's probably right. If Jane had had to go rescue you from prison she might not have been able to crack the case. Too distracting."

"Unless I become a detective, too, right?" Jake grinned.

"There is no way on God's green earth I would supervise your hours for your license, so forget that right now," Flora said. Then she sighed. "Oh, maybe I would. But not yet. Go home and think about what you've done, young man."

"Yes, ma'am."

"And give me five more minutes with Jane."

Jake stood, shook Flora's hand, then Rocky's, and left to sit around the waiting room for a few minutes.

"Good job, Jane." Flora's tone softened. "Very good job. You have a fast mind, good at puzzles, and good instincts. The more experience you get, the faster you will get at this. I'm pleased to have you on our team. Not all young detectives can do what you just did."

"Or experienced ones, either," Rocky said. "And personally, I've got hope for Jake too, if he ever decides to give up his fundraising gig."

"Before I let you go," Flora pulled another file out of her file drawer, "I have another job for you. How much do you know about felony flats?"

"What I don't know, I can learn." Jane leaned forward to have a look at the file. She might have just gotten home, but she was ready for her next case.

ABOUT THE AUTHOR

Traci Tyne Hilton is the author of The Plain Jane Mysteries, The Mitzy Neuhaus Mysteries and the Tillgiven Romantic Mysteries. She also writes short romances as Traci Valentyne Hilton.

When not writing she has been known to knit socks, play the spoons, and teach Sunday School, though these days she is most often seen in her role as taxi-driver to busy children.

She was the Mystery/Suspense Category winner for the 2012 Christian Writers of the West Phoenix Rattler Contest, a finalist for Speculative Fiction in the same contest, and has a Drammy from the Portland Civic Theatre Guild. She blogs at TheWriteConversation.blogspot.com.

Traci attended Fackelbararnas Bibelskola in Holsby Brunn, Sweden, and earned a degree in History from Portland State

University. She lives in the rainiest part of the Pacific Northwest with her husband the mandolin playing funeral director, the two busy kids, and their dogs, Dr. Watson, Archie Goodwin, and their newest addition Kitty Biscuits.

Join her at the Good Clean Book Club http://www.tracihilton.com and never miss a new release or a great deal!

Novels by Traci Tyne Hilton

The Plain Jane Mysteries

Good, Clean Murder

Dirty Little Murder

Bright New Murder

Health, Wealth, and Murder

Spoiled Rotten Murder

Killer Honeymoon

Killer Calling

The Tillgiven Romantic Mysteries

Hard to Find

Dark and Stormy

The Mitzy Neuhaus Mysteries

Foreclosed

Eminent Domain

Buyer's Remorse

Frozen Assets

Other Titles

Hearts to God

Gone: The Tangle Saga

Love and a Side of Chips